I Froze In Sudden Horror—

My murderer was in here with me. He had been watching me, until in his own chosen time he came for me. And he was coming for me now, moving as slowly as I was. As he moved he began to whisper to himself, and my heart thumped so loudly I was sure he could hear it. Then my back struck the stone wall beyond the steps and I could go no farther. I opened my mouth and screamed, and screamed again. My last hopeless shriek faded to whimpering and I felt my knees begin to buckle as he reached me. . . .

Other SIGNET books by Caroline Farr

Dark Mansion

by

Caroline Farr

A SIGNET BOOK

NEW AMERICAN LIBRARY

TIMES MIRROR

Published by arrangement with Alan G. Yates

Ⓞ SIGNET TRADEMARK REG. U.S. PAT. OFF. AND FOREIGN COUNTRIES
REGISTERED TRADEMARK——MARCA REGISTRADA
HECHO EN CHICAGO, U.S.A.

SIGNET, SIGNET CLASSICS, SIGNETTE, MENTOR AND PLUME BOOKS
are published by The New American Library, Inc.,
1301 Avenue of the Americas, New York, New York 10019

FIRST PRINTING, February, 1974

1 2 3 4 5 6 7 8 9

PRINTED IN THE UNITED STATES OF AMERICA

DARK MANSION

Chapter ONE

Sound rumbled, faintly hollow, a man grunted quietly as his foot slipped in wet clay while the rain poured down and wind whined through trees fall had already bared of leaves.

I could not force myself to watch what the grave-diggers were doing, as the others were. I kept my eyes downcast instead, staring at wet green grass and piled yellow clay blurring through the rain. The Presbyterian minister intoned the ritual faster than it seemed to me he should, but I couldn't blame him for that. I had never known my father to attend his church, though he had sent me there regularly, so they had never met. And besides, even with my eyes downcast I could see the rain-soaked legs of his trousers and those of the funeral director trying to shelter him with an umbrella while he read from his black-covered book.

The rain, driven in gusts by the wind, drummed on the taut umbrellas and upon the cedar coffin that I could not bear to look at, because that *was* my father it contained. My mind seemed to want to cling to the trancelike state that had possessed it since my father's death.

Beside me, Suanne's hand trembled on my arm, and I could hear her sobbing quietly to herself, a restrained sound I knew Suanne was trying hard to control lest she add to my distress. Neither of us had ever been to a funeral before, so I could understand the ordeal this was for her. Aside from myself, Suanne was the only person I had ever known who understood and liked him. Impressions are sharp in a girl of twenty, emotion can be devastating. I knew these things because I felt the same way, only I must stop myself from crying, because once *I* started, I'd never stop.

". . . In the hope of resurrection and life . . ."

Through the sound of wind and rain the words of the clergyman came to me intermittently, only partly understood. My father's mourners listened, as I was trying to do, with bowed heads and solemn faces. No more than a dozen friends and neighbors had gathered with Suanne and me to mourn him. A man who lived fifty years should have more friends to mourn his death, it seemed to me.

The rubber boots of the gravedigger on my side of the grave were covered in yellow clay. The feet within them moved, taking a firmer grip, straining suddenly as Suanne's hand tightened, hurting my arm so that involuntarily I glanced up and saw what she saw and stared in the same fascinated horror. The men were lowering the coffin into the grave; but it was listing badly, starting to slip from the ropes they held while they tried desperately to right it.

It was the clay! It coated the bottom of the coffin and the ropes greasily. I saw the rope nearest me flip clear, and turned my face away instinctively, not wanting to see it happen. Only Suanne and I stood here close to the clergyman; the others had grouped around the foot of the grave. I was seeing their familiar faces clearly for the first time this day. Mr. Padillo, from the corner delicatessen, was staring with horrified eyes, his hand instinctively crossing himself like the good Catholic he was. The others were all neighbors from the apartment house where we lived, or from the street in St. John, New Brunswick, where the apartment house stood.

I heard the coffin fall heavily then, and beside me Suanne cried out softly: "Oh *no!*"

Clods disturbed by the fall rained down upon it, thumping hollowly. The clergyman's voice said sharply, "No! Let it be, man!"

In self-defense I stared blindly ahead. The voice of the clergyman was continuing as calmly as though nothing had happened. The two gravediggers moved into my line of vision; they walked together to one of the leafless trees and sheltered there, waiting; and near them, standing beside a gleaming black car, I noticed for the first time the stranger at my father's funeral.

At first I thought he was Professor Spicer, my father's closest friend, even though Professor Spicer had called to tell me regretfully that he would be out of town and could not come. They'd gone bowling together, and played chess in the apartment sometimes, though my father was never in the same class as Professor Spicer as a chess player.

This man in the expensive raincoat beside the luxury car had gray hair as thick as Professor Spicer's and a body of the same solid build, but he stood there alone, bare-headed in the rain and barely conscious of its fall as he stared back at me, unsmiling, grim. There was something sinister about the man, or perhaps about his being there, that frightened me instinctively.

"Let us pray. . . ."

All my father's neighbors and friends bowed their heads obediently. I stared at the stranger, puzzling. He was watching me intently as though *I* and not my father or his funeral was his only interest here. Yet I had never seen him before. Never. He had never visited our apartment, nor had I ever seen him in my father's company. My father had never spoken of any-

one like this sinister but well-dressed man with his
great, gleaming automobile. . . .

"Our Father, Who art in heaven . . ."

The voices of my father's mourners rose, joining the
prayer, while I bowed my head, instinctively repeating
words my father had taught me long ago. But behind
my closed eyes I could still see the stranger. He had
smiled when the coffin fell; I was sure of it. A cruel
smile, it had seemed. As though he stared at someone
or something he *hated*. . . .

I stumbled in my prayer, confused. Beside me,
Suanne's clear young voice encouraged me. There was
a different sound in the responding voices now, a sound
almost of relief that brought me realization that the
end of the ritual must be approaching. I was alone
now, a girl of nineteen without money or a career,
who must suddenly fend for herself. Thoughts of the
stranger fled before a greater fear that had barely
occurred to me before. How *could* I keep myself now
that I was alone? Throughout high school and during
the one year I had spent at college it had seemed
to me that the quiet life my father and I shared in our
rented apartment would just go on and on. . . .

I would never see my father again. . . .

I was crying suddenly, crying bitterly for the first
time since his death, the tears streaming down silently
while a distressed Suanne tried desperately to comfort
me, and my breast heaved with every sob.

"You must try not to distress yourself, Miss Craig."
The clergyman moved to comfort me, the ritual over.
Some of the mourners were hurrying back to the cars,
eager to be out of the rain. Others stared at me,
embarrassed. He had a deep, sincere voice, and he
was trying to hold the umbrella over himself and
comfort me at the same time. "Pray for strength and
peace, and God will comfort you. Let me help you to

your car. We're still all getting wet, you know. Such an unhappy days. . . ."

I shook my head and stood fast. "Thank you, Reverend, but I can't leave yet. Not till they're finished."

He hesitated, studying me. "My dear girl, if it was the slight accident the men had with the ropes, I assure you there was no damage done. You should go home now. Go home with Suanne and have something hot to drink. In weather like this, you could get pneumonia."

The gravediggers were coming back. I said, "Suanne can go, Reverend. I mean to stay until they've finished whatever they still have to do."

He found a damp handkerchief and wiped rain from his face. "Would you like *me* to stay with you, Tracey?"

"I'll stay with her, Reverend," Suanne volunteered

I shook my head. "Suanne, please go. I want you both to . . . just go."

"All they can do in this weather is place canvas over the grave and put the flowers on it," the clergyman said practically. "They don't complete their work till everyone is gone. They used to, but it took too long and was too distressing for relatives. Tracey, you're a modern young woman; you must realize the common sense in that?"

"Just for a little while I . . . want to be alone with him."

"Then it isn't just that you want to see the burial through?"

"No."

"I'll stay and pray *with* you, Tracey," he said gently, as though he had discovered in me a religious quality he hadn't suspected existed.

"No."

He shook his head. "You're a stubborn girl. Suanne, leave her your umbrella. I'll shelter you to the cars."

"I don't want to leave her!" Suanne's eyes welled, looking at me.

The clergyman put his hand on Suanne's arm, leading her away.

"I'll wait for you in the car," Suanne muttered.

The gravediggers started unwrapping a folded tarpaulin. I heard the clergyman say in a low, reassuring voice, "She won't stay there long, Suanne. Not *alone*."

The men working kept glancing at me resentfully, but with a morbid curiosity. Cars started, pulling away in the rain. I glimpsed faces watching me as they left. A few hands raised in farewell, but I took no notice. The workmen displayed the flowers quickly and carelessly upon the green tarpaulin, and they too hurried away through the rain. The wet flowers looked alive and growing.

Now, I thought, I can say good-bye, Dad.

I'm not sure how long I stood there, Suanne's umbrella forgotten in my hand. But I kept seeing my father as I had known him, pipe-smoking, quiet, but always kind and generous to me within his power. I remembered him best sitting behind his desk in one cramped corner of our living room, picking out words on a battered typewriter. Words he never seemed able to sell to any publisher, no matter how he tried. He had tried for twenty years to build a career as a writer upon one small successful novel and a few published short stories. He had not succeeded. I remembered only two short stories that he had published while I was at high school.

I knew now that my father had never been a good writer. He could compose beautiful prose, but it rarely said anything. His characters were the same unreal, idealistic ghosts, formed within the narrow confines of the space where he worked. He had never mixed enough, I had long ago decided. He was dead now, but to my knowledge of him while we were together, he had never really lived.

Yet maybe, I thought now, that was not *his* fault. For we had eaten and paid our rent. We had worn decent clothes, and he had educated me. If I needed extra money, he gave it to me. I'd never known him to refuse me anything, even if it meant going without himself. But where his money came from, I had no idea. It was not in his bank account, for there had not been enough there, when I searched, to pay for the modest funeral. The balance of that debt had emptied my small savings account built up from pocket money at high school.

All I knew of his source of income was that his bank books showed that on the first day of each month a sum of less than three hundred dollars was paid into the account from some undisclosed source. On a yearly basis that barely gave us a living. But it had kept him writing, when he could have turned his energy into more profitable channels. I blamed this for what had happened to him. And for what was happening to me now. For where the next month's rent of the apartment was to come from, I had no way of knowing—unless the regular payments he had received all my life still came in, and could be transferred to me.

I sighed and came back to the present. It had been a late funeral, and dusk would come early this evening. It was already becoming gloomy beneath the leafless trees, and on the highway beyond the cemetery the car lights were coming on. I decided that none of my worries were really my father's fault, and chances were I was better equipped to handle life than he had been. Even starting broke.

At least I no longer seemed afraid to face what lay ahead.

It occurred to me suddenly that perhaps my father had tried just before he died to explain the source of his income, and to advise me about it. But I would never be sure about that now. I had found him lying where he had fallen from the chair behind his desk when I returned from an evening lecture.

He was paralyzed and couldn't talk. Only his eyes were terribly, desperately alive in a once-handsome face twisted into a grimace. He seemed trying desperately to keep me with him. His lips writhed, trembling as he seemed to be holding death at bay in order to disclose something to me. I could not raise his heavy body, nor in my state of shock understand what he was trying to tell me. In the end I panicked and ran screaming for help to the neighbors, and fainted outside the Todd apartment when Suanne opened the door. My father had lapsed into unconsciousness before we got back.

He died without regaining consciousness. Whatever he had wanted to say was lost forever now.

I had been living those terrible moments over again, standing beside his grave in the falling rain. I shivered suddenly with cold and became aware that, in remembering, I had started crying again. But this was no place to linger upon memories with darkness coming early through the windblown rain. I glanced back apprehensively at the gravel drive and saw that only the black limousine, which was the only funeral car I could afford, still waited there.

"Good-bye Dad!" I whispered, and pulled my raincoat close and walked away.

I had not realized till then how wet I was, or how cold the rain. I hurried through the puddles to the waiting car, struggling to get the umbrella down as I got into the back seat.

"I'm sorry, Suanne!" I muttered. "I shouldn't have kept you waiting so long in the cold!"

"I sent her home in the other car, Miss Craig," the driver said.

"Oh?" I was more surprised than pleased, I think, that Suanne had left me. Although I had no right to expect more, since she must've been almost as wet as I. "Did she go home with Mr. Padillo, then?"

I shook the water from the umbrella and closed the door. The driver had said something, but doing these things, I hadn't heard.

"I'm sorry, what was that you said?"

"I sent her home in the car you hired, Miss Craig," he said turning his head toward me. "I told her I'd drive you home, because there are matters I must discuss with you that must be decided tonight."

"You what?" I turned in dismay to stare at him, and my heart started a sick pounding born of fright as I recognized the shock of thick gray hair, the sardonic face of the stranger I had stared at across my father's grave. . . .

"I said there are things I must discuss with you that can't wait until tomorrow, Miss Craig. So I sent your friend home. Shall we discuss these matters at your apartment? Or can you suggest some other place? I don't know anyone in St. John, other than you."

"I don't know you," I said, trying to keep my voice steady. "Who are you?" The lights were on along the drive. A car passed, going toward the gates, lights on and wipers busy. Beyond his head, the stark branches of a tree moved in the wind, silhouetted against one of the lights along the drive. There was no other movement when the car had gone. It occurred to me that now I was alone with this man in his big car. That ours was the last car in the cemetery.

For a moment he seemed to consider what I had said, and I thought he was not going to answer. I remembered that the door by which I had entered was not locked. My hand reached stealthily for the handle as he bent toward the ignition as though to start the car. In another moment I would have been out and running in panic through the rain and the darkness, but the dome light overhead came to life instead of the motor, and he seemed less frightening in the brighter light.

"My name can mean nothing to you," he said. "However, your father's handwriting must. Can you recognize it in this light?" His harsh voice had a Scottish accent, unmistakable to me, because even after eighteen years in New Brunswick, my father had never quite lost his.

"Of course." I frowned suspiciously. "Are you saying my father wrote to you? He never mentioned that to me."

"No doubt there are many things he never mentioned to you, young lady," he said sardonically. "But I never said he wrote to me. He wrote to someone else, enclosing this envelope which carries an instruction that seems to me self-explanatory. Wouldn't you agree?"

He was offering me a manila envelope taken from his pocket, one of the kind in which for years my father's manuscripts had traveled to and from the publishers.

I examined it suspiciously beneath the dome light. "It looks like my father's handwriting," I conceded reluctantly at last.

"There's Craig blood in you," he said. "Your caution reminds me of it. But can you read what's written there? Because it's time we were out of here. It's possible they lock the gates at night."

The thought appalled me. I read hastily, something I'd neglected to do in my concern with the way the writer formed his letters. I read it aloud.

" 'In the event that it has not been opened previously or destroyed by my brother John Craig, this letter is to be opened only by Mr. Angus McDonald, attorney-at-law, of Aberfeld, Nova Scotia, Canada, in the presence of my daughter, Tracey Craig, of 5 Borden Street, St. John, New Brunswick, Canada, and subsequently read and explained to her as I believe only Mr. McDonald can, as witness my hand and seal, Henry Craig.' " I looked up at him puzzling. "Is this my father's will?"

He took the envelope back before he shook his head and frowned. "I know no more what's inside than you do," he said gruffly, putting it back in his pocket. "But his will—no, I wouldn't think so. Your father had nothing to leave, young lady."

"He was always kind to me," I declared, coming quickly to his defense. "He gave me what he could afford. He never refused me anything. He was a good man, Mr. McDonald, if that's really your name?"

"Oh, it's really my name," he said. "And that's easy enough to prove, should you demand it. Now, shall we get away from this dismal place while we can? I have a suite booked at the Admiral Beatty Hotel. We could go there."

"We'll go to my apartment," I said. "I'll show you the way."

"I know the way," he said, turning back to his controls. "You'll find my card beneath your door, with the hotel phone number. You were gone when I reached your apartment. I was only told of this last night, and it's a long drive. Your father never did have much sense of time."

"You knew him, then?" I said, surprised.

"I knew him," he said. The car came purring to life, and we moved off. Riding in his car was like floating on a cloud.

He never made a mistake or missed a turn until we pulled in to the curb outside the entrance on Borden Street.

I stirred reluctantly from the deeply cushioned seat. "You have a good sense of direction," I said, opening my own door.

"I have a good memory," he said. "I was here this morning, as I told you." He came around the car to lock my door carefully. Outside the apartment the gleaming black sedan seemed a block long. A couple I recognized going into an apartment house across the street stopped to stare at it. At another time I might have appreciated their interest, but I was exhausted and wet, drained of emotion. I wanted only to be rid of this man with the stern, unfriendly face.

I said as we climbed the steps to the entrance, "My father never told me he had a brother."

He glanced at me, peering from beneath heavy, graying brows. "He had reason."

"His brother spent twenty years hating him," he said gruffly.

"Why?" I demanded.

He shook his head.

"You mean, you don't know why?"

"Oh, I know, well enough," he said. "But telling it to you is another thing. Your father seems to believe that he can trust me to do what's best for you. Though why he should is beyond my understanding, since for twenty years I've had little more time for him than his brother has."

I bristled instinctively. "My father could never have been mean to anyone. You admitted yourself that he was a good man. What did he do to make you or anyone else hate him?"

He gave me a resentful glance. "Don't tempt me, girl. It's not in your best interests to learn it."

I stopped abruptly. "Yet you're prepared to damn my father to me with insinuations."

"I parried your questions—that's all," he growled, angered.

"You hint that he did something wrong. Something shameful enough to make his brother hate him. And you appear to agree with that hatred; therefore, you must believe that my father did whatever it was."

His lips tightened as he studied me, and he shook his head. "You'll not get it from me that way, girl," he said sourly. "Nor trap me with your silly questioning."

"I'm not sure that I want to have anything to do with you, Mr. McDonald," I told him bitterly.

"That was never *my* wish," he said. "It was your father's. Remember his instruction? The envelope I showed you may only be opened by me in your presence. Otherwise I have no option but to return it to John Craig, who will destroy it as any right-minded man would have done in the first place the moment he received it."

"Then you *do* that!" I told him angrily, and suddenly it was all too much for me, so that the tears came flooding back, blinding me. I found my key, but could not get it in the lock with tears streaming down. Hands as strong as iron took hold of my fingers and prized the key away from me. He opened the door and followed me inside. He stared around disapprovingly while I tried to find words to be rid of him.

"So this is where Henry Craig kept you?" he muttered, shaking his head disgustedly. "A poor place compared with what you might have had."

"I like it here. . . . Please . . . just *go!*" I sobbed.

He glanced at me. "On second thought I've brought this message too far to take it back unread," he said. "Or be diverted by any childish whim of yours." He took the envelope from his pocket and felt its thickness, staring down at it from beneath scowling gray brows. "This contains no more than a single sheet of paper. Ten minutes, and we can be rid of each other."

"I . . . told you to *go!*"

"If his message is what I suspect it must be to your advantage to hear it," he said. "I feel obliged to tell you that." He looked at me directly again; scowling. "Well, what d'you say?"

I hesitated, wanting only to be rid of him, but remembering how desperately my father had tried to tell me something as he lay dying in the corner of this room where we stood. Had he thought of some way of helping me by writing to a brother he had never allowed me to know existed? A brother this man said hated him?

"Well?" he demanded impatiently.

"Wait here" I muttered. In the bathroom I turned the key in the lock against the threat of his presence before I began to bathe my tear-stained face. As I patted my eyes with cold water, I heard him moving about outside as though inspecting the apartment, muttering to himself disapprovingly as he did so. When I came out at last, red-eyed, he had settled behind my father's desk in my father's chair, the envelope on the desk before him. That was like sacrilege, angering me.

"My father worked there!" I told him indignantly. "He was sitting in that chair when he had his stroke."

He spared me a glance, and I saw him clearly for the first time. There was strength in his brown face, as there was in the wide shoulders and big, square hands. It occurred to me as I noticed locks of jet black among his gray hair that he must have been a strikingly handsome man once, for his eyes were a very dark blue that fifty or so years had been unable to fade. Mr. McDonald at twenty with jet-black hair and violet eyes could have been a dreamboat—except for his sour disposition.

"I'm not fastidious about such things," he said curtly. "Now, suppose you sit down, and we'll conclude this as quickly as we can and go our separate ways."

I fought an imminent explosion and sat down, contenting myself by telling him coldly, "That can't happen soon enough for me!"

He read without glasses, brows drawn down slightly as he reread my father's instruction before he opened the envelope and unfolded the sheet of paper within. He cleared his throat and glanced at me.

"There is a preface addressed to me."

"Oh? Does he say *why* he wanted *you* to read it to me?"

"He expected me to help bring about what he wanted, of course," he said grimly. "The preface does not concern you. Shall I go on?"

I nodded.

"The rest of it does. He writes:

" 'To my daughter, Tracey Craig: I cannot be certain that you will receive this, my last bequest to you, because it is part of a letter to my brother John Craig in which, being unable to provide for you myself, I appealed to him to help you.

" 'I have never spoken to you of my family, or of my brother John. Years ago I did something that my family believed wronged John deeply, and the Craigs are a dour people who never forgive a wrong, even when committed by one of themselves. Because of this, my parents took away the inheritance that was mine by birth, substituting for it a fund designed for the duration of my life to give me the equivalent of the weekly wage of the lowest-paid workers in the Craig mines.

" 'With my death, that income ceases, and no provision was ever made for you.

" 'I accepted their pittance because I hoped to make a success of writing, and one day build a better life for us both than even they could give us. With success I meant to throw their charity back to them, but success eluded me. Recently my doctors informed me that I have an arterial disease which must soon prove fatal, and I find myself worrying more and more about what will happen to you when I am gone.

" 'Because of this, I have written to my brother John, now head of the Craig family. He is a strange and bitter man, and he hates me. But you have the blood of the Craigs of Aberfeld in your veins, and he cannot have any valid reason to inflict his hatred upon you. Rather, for reasons that I cannot disclose, he may even find in his bitter heart more reason to love you.

" 'If you receive this message, it will mean that John has agreed at least in part to the things I begged of him in my letter. It will also mean that Angus McDonald, a man once my close friend, is beside you. He thinks as the others do about me, but Angus is a man of great integrity, so I believe he will advise you well.

" 'Tracey, I request you—no, I *command* you—to go to Aberfeld with Angus McDonald, because in this uncertain world it is only at Aberfeld that I can see security for you.

" 'Your rightful heritage is there. Claim it.' "

Angus McDonald looked up at me, scowling. "It is

signed with his signature—which I recognize, as he expected me to do." He waited a long moment. "Well?"

I blinked back tears that those written words from my father had provoked, and gave him back his scowl. "Why should I go to a relative I've never known . . . one who hates my father?"

"Relatives," he said. "There are more Craigs than your father's brother, John. Men and women."

"Who hated Dad too, no doubt?"

He nodded. "But you ask why you should go to Aberfeld. You should go, first, because it is your father's command. And second, because, as he says and as he expected me as an attorney to verify, you *could* find security there. You are a Craig, and the Craigs are more than wealthy. You may even, as he deviously suggests, have some small claim on the Craig estate which John Craig administers. I will go so far as to check on that for you." He unfolded a small penknife he had taken from his pocket and carefully cut away the preface from my father's letter and gave me the other part.

"Do *you* think I should go to Aberfeld?" I muttered.

"If you were my client, I would advise it."

I shook my head. "I can't go to Aberfeld, even if I wanted to. It's in Nova Scotia, it said on the envelope you showed me. I don't have the fare."

He looked shocked. "So you're as improvident as he was? Nothing saved?"

"I had several hundred dollars saved," I retorted, stung. "I've saved what I could from my allowance ever since I started school."

"Then use that."

"It went on the funeral you attended today."

He glanced around, scowling, and muttered something too low for me to hear. He said aloud, "The estate would stop his allowance automatically with his death, of which our branch office in St. John advised us. And this apartment was rented furnished. There's nothing left. . . ."

"He had money saved. But today took almost all we both had." It was worse than that. There was a balance still left to pay, and other small debts, but I wasn't going to tell *him* that.

"You have no choice," he said. "You go with me in my car to Aberfeld—where you belong. . . ."

Chapter *TWO*

In the end it was the Todds, husband and wife and a tearful Suanne, who persuaded me I should go to Aberfeld with dour Mr. Angus McDonald. He had business to transact, he informed me as we drove out of St. John, with me still furtively dabbing at my eyes; there were matters he must attend to in both Pictou and Antigonish in Nova Scotia. It seemed he was a busy man as well as a surly and silent one.

Mostly we drove with him glowering at the road ahead and paying me no more attention than he did the passing scene. But *I* had that to interest me as we drove. I had never been beyond Moncton in my native New Brunswick, where the great tides rushing up the Petitcodiac drew tourists from all over, like our own Reversing Falls of St. John, where the same mighty tides of Fundy force a twenty-six-foot waterfall to climb back uphill.

Nova Scotia was new to me, like and yet unlike New Brunswick. We passed through Scottish communities that seemed more Scottish to me than the Highlands could be, French communities more French than Normandy. While Mr. McDonald transacted his business in Pictou, I wandered through the town to the wharves, where scores of lobster boats were tied up. The crews mending their cane traps spoke broader Scotch than Mr. McDonald or my father, and the names proudly displayed over shops and cafés were Scottish to a man.

We stayed overnight in a hotel, where Mr. McDonald

was most careful to explain that I was *not* his daughter nor any other relative, and to ask as carefully for rooms at opposite ends of the passage.

It was the same at Antigonish, farther east, where his business made it necessary to stay another night before driving to Cape Breton Island and Aberfeld. In one of his more expansive moments as we drove through valleys where apple orchards were losing their leaves, he confided that Highland Games were held in Antigonish each July, and you'd see more kilts worn there than in Scotland.

We drove across a causeway to Cape Breton Island from the mainland of Nova Scotia. And suddenly it seemed we were in a different world, a Scottish Highland world of misty glens and brooding moors, where deep lakes reflected the weak autumn sunshine on mirror surfaces. The place names changed from French to Scottish, so that we passed through villages and towns with Gaelic names like Skir Dhu and Beinn Dearg, Crieff and Ingonish, and more that I've forgotten.

For seventy miles or more we drove past scenery as starkly beautiful as the Highlands I'd seen pictured in my father's books, now stored at the Todds' apartment. There were even the same sturdy, long-haired Highland cattle staring at us truculently from hillside farms on either side, and once, as we passed through forest, a deer with great branching antlers stared at us quite unafraid.

The country became wilder, the ranges higher. The cattle we saw fled in fright as we approached. I began to notice the ruins of old timber buildings on the high slopes.

"What are they?" I asked, pointing.

"Mines," he told me gruffly. "Coal mines. Those

were abandoned when the seams worked out. We still have mines working, but far from here."

"Then, these were Craig mines?" I stared, astonished, at the empty lands with only a few cattle to be seen, near the broken timbers of an old pithead. I added, awed, "Was all this once Craig land?"

"This is still Craig land," he said. "And profitable. The coal is finished, but the land still produces profitably. Beef, lamb, lumber from the back country up in the hills."

"And all this belongs to my father's family?"

He smiled coldly. "To your family, Miss Craig. You've been driving over Craig lands for the past five miles, and will for the next five before you reach Craig Glamis and Aberfeld."

"Craig Glamis?"

"So the Craig home is called."

I frowned, remembering, not wanting to let him lapse back into the silence from which he had emerged only with monosyllabic replies for many miles. "Wasn't Glamis supposed to be the home of Shakespeare's Macbeth?"

"Macbeth was Thane of Glamis and King of Scotland from 1039 till 1056; when he was killed in battle against a combined Scottish and English army fighting to restore the throne to King Duncan's son, Malcolm. The records prove this, though not the English poet's fancies. The Craig lairds and their clans followed Macbeth."

"I thought *all* that was fiction." I studied his unsmiling profile. "The McDonalds followed the Craigs, of course?"

His glance at me was coldly hostile. "What makes you think so?"

I shrugged. "You follow them blindly in other things, like the way you feel about my father."

"Never blindly," he said. "Then, or now. The Mc-Donalds were lairds in Scotland long before the usurper Macbeth came to the throne, or the Craigs were more than poor herdsmen and crofters. We fought for Malcolm, King Duncan's son, against Macbeth and the Craigs. We helped Malcolm to the throne and kept him there thirty years while he ruled Scotland, as was his right."

He turned back to his driving while I tried to find a less controversial subject. But I had already lost him. The country was changing again; there were more fences, a dairy farm where a man driving cows into a barn waved as though he recognized the car. Mr. McDonald took no notice of him, so I sighed and settled back. As we climbed a ridge, I began to glimpse smoke ahead. We crossed the crest, and below us was a town.

"Aberfeld," he said. "Craig Glamis stands there on the cliffs above it. The Craigs built Glamis strong. There was fighting here then, both with the French and with the Americans. Aberfeld was taken twice, but never Glamis."

"I can see why," I said. "It's beautiful, and yet . . ." I left it unsaid, aware of fear as I stared down a long hill at this great stone mansion behind massive walls built upon a cliff that jutted out into a cold green sea that leaped and growled beneath it.

Glamis was built of very dark stone bonded in lighter-colored stone at the corners. The roof was flat and turreted like the castle of some medieval robber baron. The windows were small and inaccessible, and I could see slits in the outer walls designed also for their defense.

"And yet what?" he asked, glancing at me.

"It's . . . scary," I muttered.

"That was its purpose," he said. "To frighten off

potential attackers. Later, the first Craig mine was sunk there, behind those walls. The seams of coal that made the Craigs wealthy were first noticed in the cliff face beneath Craig Glamis. The mine shafts run for miles below the sea. They're abandoned now, and extremely dangerous. It's an eerie place down there, with the earth enclosing you, and the sea above. In some shafts, sound carries through the rock in bad weather, so that you can hear the sea smashing against the cliffs above you."

"No, thank you!" I said, shuddering. "I hate confined spaces anywhere. But down there . . .!"

"Well, I hardly expect anyone to tempt you to take a walk beneath the sea," he said. "Nobody has been down there for years now. Nor will again, in their right senses."

The town was larger than I expected. We drove past rows of well-kept cottages built of the same dark stone as Craig Glamis and bonded in the same way. The slate roofs had a lacing of gray-white lichens, and Aberfeld could have been a Tudor village of long ago. White lace curtains showed at windows where old-fashioned painted shutters stood open to the sunlight.

We turned, going a little out of our way, I thought, to drive along Aberfeld's main street. The houses became shops with the same old-world appearance and display windows no larger than those of the houses.

"My office is next to the hotel," he said, nodding at it as we drove past. "My grandfather opened up here nearly a century ago. Our head office is in Halifax, but we've a number of equally important branches, notably in Quebec and Montreal."

"You've done well with the Craigs?" I said, slightly sarcastic.

"Or without them."

A girl in a miniskirt wearing a figure-molding

jumper came out of the building next door, bringing
me back from Tudor times abruptly to the present.
Some burly, red-haired man wearing kilt, jacket, and
broadsword would've been more appropriate. Behind
her I noticed the brass plate at the entrance: Dr. Peter
McDonald, M.D., FRCS.

"Another McDonald?" I asked.

"My son," he said. "And a disappointment to me,
since he chose medicine instead of law. He's unmarried,
and could be the last of our family unless he does
something about it. He's the only child my wife and I
have."

I smiled. "It's a wonder you haven't married him to
a Craig. You told me in St. John that there are girls
at Glamis, didn't you?"

"*A* girl," he said. "Your cousin, Sandra Craig. But
young men like to make their own choice, and he's
never shown the slightest interest in your cousin. Or in
any girl in Aberfeld, if it comes to that. Still, what you
suggest might not be such a bad idea." The glance he
gave me was oddly speculative, embarrassing me.

If he thought *I* could be interested in a son of *his*,
he was crazy! Why, he'd done nothing but frighten
and annoy me since I first saw him standing in the
rain—a sinister, unknown figure on the opposite side
of my father's grave. Chances were his son was just
like him! I retreated into silence as we left the town
behind and drove along a graveled road that climbed
toward the distant walls of Glamis upon its lonely cliff.

With a good paved road through the Craig lands,
the gravel road leading to the Craig mansion seemed
out of place, until I found reason for it in the rusted
steel lines of the railroad that had once moved coal
from the mines. The small railroad still formed the
edge of the road, its ties embedded in gravel, the steel
lines rusting but still firmly secured. It would be quite a

chore replacing the old railroad with a paved road, and I supposed it could cost plenty.

I wanted to ask Mr. McDonald why, when the Craigs apparently had plenty of money, they hadn't decided to do something about it. But I was still angry, so I stared sullenly ahead at the entrance to Glamis, where massive iron gates stood open. Mr. McDonald had slowed, for there was barely room for our car to get through between the near rail and the hewn stone of the cut we were approaching.

Beyond the cut I could see the great wall of Glamis curving toward the sea around a network of rusting railroad lines where derelict coal cars from the mines beneath the sea now stood in untidy rows, slowly rusting away. It seemed a waste of material, rails, ties, and cars that, to my mind, might have been used elsewhere if the Craigs had other mines working. Only, suddenly, then I noticed that one of the cars up there was moving slowly, as though being pushed by someone straining behind it.

"They would have paved this road long ago," Mr. McDonald said. "But the mining engineers found new coal seams not far from here, and decided to leave the railroad where it is until they'd been tested. The tests were completed a year or so ago, and found uneconomical, but your uncle hasn't got around to doing anything about the road yet. The rolling stock you're looking at is useless now. Hasn't moved in years. And it wouldn't pay to take up and transport the rails, even if someone had a use for them."

"You're wrong about the cars not moving," I said. "One of them is. A man had to push to get it started, but it *is* moving."

"Impossible," he said.

I looked for the railroad car, checking. It was still moving; only, by itself now. The man had gone back

among the other stationary trucks. I watched him move
in among them, then stop and begin tugging at a lever
of some sort. The railroad car was moving faster now
on lines angling across the slope toward the road beyond the cutting.

"Look for yourself," I said. "And don't tell me the
railroad car isn't moving. It is, and going faster now."

"Did you say someone pushed it?"

"That's right. He went back among the other cars.
Maybe he's going to move some more of them. He was
pulling some kind of lever there, the last time I saw
him." I searched, but he had disappeared. I said, "I
can't see him now, but you must be able to see the
railroad car. . . ."

He saw it suddenly. *"My God, girl!"* he cried, and
our right wheel jammed against the near rail hard, and
the big car, moving at slow speed as it was, promptly
stalled. Momentarily he froze over the wheel staring up
the steep slope as I was; then he was jabbing at the
starter. The railroad car had reached the road; it
swayed for a moment, and I was sure that it must
overturn, but it made the turn; and picking up speed
with every yard, now it was coming straight down the
hill at us. I stared, appalled, realizing for the first time
what was happening. That steel triangular-shaped coal
car bearing down upon us at ever-increasing speed must
overhang the nearest rail by a good two feet. And our
automobile wheels on the passenger's side, where I sat,
had been brushing the rail. If the coal-car projectile
hurling itself at me hit the automobile, it must sheer
away the side where I sat—*and shear me away with it!*

That was *death* I was watching bearing down upon
me, while Mr. McDonald started the car and pressed
the accelerator. I shrieked in dismay as the car lurched
forward instead of backward as I expected.

"What are you doing?" I cried in terror, grip
seat.

"Be quiet!" he hissed.

We were going faster suddenly, the big car surging forward, scraping the rail on one side or the hewn rock of the cut on the other every few yards—but rushing to meet that runaway coal car now as fast as it was rushing at us. The end of the cut was coming up. I glimpsed green grass on either side ahead, but had eyes only for that steel coal car, looking huge and more deadly now as it closed upon us. Its wheels shrieked from the speed of turning grinding metal upon metal, while smoke and sparks streamed from its tortured axles. The trapdoor in its side, designed to pour coal from it when working, had come unstuck and was flogging its side, up and down, unmercifully, and with a hellish clatter.

Rocking uncertainly upon lines no longer safe to hold it, the coal car rushed upon us. That flailing door was an added, terrible danger, I knew. And the coal car *was* going to hit us! *Must hit us now!*

My eyes closed instinctively at the last moment. I grabbed desperately for someone, something, *anything to cling to!* Something struck our automobile a giant, hammer blow. We swerved violently. I screamed in abject terror as I was flung from my seat, as I felt my seat belt give and fall away. Momentarily I had the sensation of flying; then my teeth jarred together as something struck my head and I fell into a bottomless, horrifying darkness. . . .

I was lying on crushed green grass, for I could smell it, and someone was trying to make me drink some spirit that was too strong and made me cough as it filled my mouth and nostrils with its fumes.

"The fool girl would've been all right if she hadn't pulled her door open and undone her seat belt," a said disgustedly. "As it was, she ar like a cork from a bottle. But I when she did no more than roll downhill ass."

's coming out of it now, Dad. She fainted, that's a.. No damage except for a few bruises on her body."

"You'd better get her up to the house," Angus Mc-Donald's voice said. "Take her in your car, Peter, then come back for me. I'll send someone from Aberfeld to tow the car home."

"Not till I look at that cut on your head."

My head stopped swimming slowly, and I opened my eyes and took a peep. Angus McDonald was squatting on grass not far from me, while a tall young man put adhesive tape over a cut on the side of his forehead. The tape gave the attorney a rakish look.

A leather case open on the grass beside them had "Peter McDonald, M.D." on it in gold letters, and I'd been right about the son being like his father. He looked as I'd imagined Angus McDonald in his twenties. He had the lean build of an athlete, and his father's almost violet eyes, and thick, jet-black hair. Although undeniably very handsome, he probably had his father's mean disposition too, like everything else.

"You might give *me* some of that," Mr. McDonald said grumpily. "You gave *her* some."

"You didn't faint," his son said, but he put some of the amber spirit into a medicine glass and gave it to him anyway. "How d'you think the truck got onto this downhill grade?"

"*She* said she saw someone pushing it," the attorney growled. "But I can't believe that. She saw it moving— but she imagined the man. There wasn't anyone in the old marshaling yards that *I* could see. If someone started the damned thing rolling, or even noticed what was happening, why didn't they come down to help us?"

"The wheels must be so rusted onto the axles, nobody could start them moving by just pushing. And the points. They'd be so rusted that the car couldn't turn down the main track."

"But the car *did* turn down here. And there *was* a man up there," I muttered, still feeling faint.

They both looked at me quickly, and Peter McDonald got up and came over. "You must rest for a while," he said soothingly. "I'm a doctor. You fainted and were thrown from the car, but fortunately you were only slightly bruised. You were very lucky. Both of you!"

"Right now I don't feel lucky," I muttered. "I just feel sick and sore! And you're both wrong. There was a man up there. And he did start the coal car by pushing it. I saw him do that. When it was moving by itself, he hurried back among the other cars."

"Before Dad saw him?" he asked, frowning.

"That's right. He stopped where I could still see him and started pulling some kind of lever. I don't know why. I told Mr. McDonald he was there, but when I tried to show him the man, he had gone. After that, all either of us saw was that thing hurtling down the hill at us!" I shuddered, remembering.

"Some kind of *lever*?" Peter McDonald said, glancing at his father. "Dad, that could be the points switch. There has to be one there to open the way into the downgrade."

"Couldn't someone have greased these things to make them work?" I asked, trying to sit up.

The son moved at once to help me, and I was glad of the support of his arm, even while I protested that I didn't need it.

"I suppose someone could have been working on the car and the switch," he said. "Dad, what do you think?"

"I hope you realize what this implies," his father said grumpily, getting up. "That someone has been greasing wheels and switches to let a car run down the hill. If there *was* someone working up there, he would have been able to see us coming from the village. He must've known we were in the cutting when he started the car rolling and threw the switch."

"Now, wait, Dad," Peter McDonald said, his glance at me embarrassed. "He may not have seen the car. It could have been accidental."

"The implication is that a premeditated attempt has been made to kill us," his father said. "I can't accept that. Not having any enemies in Aberfeld, I prefer to suspect that gravity started a coal car moving downhill, to a switch that has stood open . . . maybe for years." He gave me an angry glare. "Or do you have the kind of enemies who might want to kill you, Miss Craig— and wouldn't shed tears if an innocent party was killed at the same time?"

"You know as well as I do you're the only person I know here," I told him stiffly.

"That's right," he said. "And since I drove the car, I have a good alibi."

Peter McDonald glanced from his father to me, frowning. He said slowly, "If someone *has* been working on the rolling stock, John Craig will know of it. He'll send someone to check. If the switch was greased, there should still be grease on it, and on the wheels and axles of the smashed coal car. But that can wait on getting you both to Glamis. We'll use the other road."

"I wish I'd used it in the first place," his father said ruefully. "I would still have my own car to drive."

Peter McDonald started helping me up gently. I discovered that I had been wrapped in a raincoat that I recognized as that of his father. I started around curiously, his hand on my arm steadying me. The car I had traveled in stood just clear of the cut, slewed back the way it had come, with the back fender on my side looking as though it had been hacked through with an ax. I shuddered, remembering that flailing iron door of the coal car rushing at me.

"I'm sorry about your lovely car, Mr. McDonald!" I said.

"The thing is, we're both unharmed," he said gruffly. "And you with your life before you. The car does not matter. It can be repaired, or I'll buy another. But it was too damned close for comfort. Far too close!"

He stared up the hill toward the open gates of Craig Glamis, his blue eyes glinting suddenly, almost black. It was a look of anger that startled me. It occurred to me with the shock of suspicion that even if he had *not* seen the man up there, he suspected who he was!

He caught me watching him. He smiled thinly and shook his head. The expression I thought I had seen was gone, if it had ever existed.

With his hand on my arm and his son on the other side of me, I was being walked toward a small parked car that I hadn't noticed before, which stood on a lesser but safer gravel road leading to the open gates of Craig Glamis. . . .

Chapter *THREE*

I stared around curiously as we drove through the open gates of Craig Glamis. Several acres of lawns and red-gravel drives, walks, and squares were laid out with mathematical precision, sprouting shrubs shaped as chess pieces. There were no flowerbeds or flowers, nor any flowering tree or shrub that I could see. The red gravel was the only contrast to the green of incredibly smooth lawns already touched by the first mild frosts of fall, lawns that must soon brown and disappear beneath the snows of late fall and winter.

The great house faced us, gloomy in dark stone despite the lighter decorative Tudor bonding at its corners. On its left a smaller building stood apart, joined to the great stone wall that protected Glamis on that side from the sea. The effect of the mansion and its grounds against a background of heavy cloud I found grim and suddenly frightening, so that I found myself wishing I hadn't listened to the advice of Angus McDonald to come to Craig Glamis. If I could have gone home at that moment, I would've done so, no matter what anyone here thought or said.

But it was too late for that. Following Mr. McDonald's instructions, the apartment was closed now, my father's few possessions sold or given to charity. I sighed and allowed Peter McDonald to help me out of his two-door car, while he smiled reassuringly as though he saw the doubt in my mind.

"They'll be surprised to see me back," he said, pull-

ing the seat forward to let his father out. "I was just
leaving when I saw the accident. Your Uncle John has
a heart condition that needs regular examinations. But
you know that."

"She knows nothing of Glamis or its people," his
father said gruffly. He climbed out while his son held
the seat forward, complaining under his breath at the
cramped space and his stiffness.

"I suppose you let them know from Antigonish that
she would arrive today?"

"I left a message for John Craig with Mrs. Brunier
before I left here, informing him I expected to return
today. I had other things on my mind in Antigonish
last night and this morning. Craig Investments are not
my only clients, just as the Craig family are not *your*
only patients, Peter," his father said irritably.

Waiting for them, I stared up at Glamis, rising three
stories above me beyond semicircular stone steps worn
by age. The great doors were closed; the small, high
windows disclosed nothing of what lay beyond them.
There certainly seemed no welcoming committee await-
ing me here. I had the feeling that when the McDonalds
left, I would lose my only remaining friends.

The closer I got to the great doors, climbing the
steps with Peter McDonald's hand on my arm, the
stronger my feeling of foreboding became. A bell pealed
distantly as Peter rang. The sound, made melancholy
by distance, added to the burden of my apprehension.

"Shall I see either of you again?" I asked with forced
cheerfulness to break the silence that was increasing
my nervousness. "If not . . . thank you both for what
you've done for me."

"You'll see me again, Miss Craig." Peter smiled.
"Tomorrow morning, when I call here to make sure
there are no side effects. And after that, no doubt we'll
meet on my regular house calls, or in the village, when

you happen to be there. Unless you prefer another doctor?"

"Is there another doctor in Aberfeld?"

"Frankly, no," he said, grinning. "Fortunately."

I noticed the way his father was studying his expression, and looked away. I knew what Angus McDonald was thinking. I remembered what he had said about his son, Peter, not showing any interest in girls here or at Aberfeld. Peter seemed to be showing more than just professional interest in me. I stole a glance at Peter, and he was even more handsome than I had thought. . . .

"Then you seem to be stuck with me as a patient," I said.

"Hmm," he said doubtfully. "I'm not so sure I meant that wholly in a professional sense. We *do* have some social life here, you know. And dances, clambakes, lobstering, and a few other peculiarly local participation sports can be fun. Even your cousins take part in them at times. After all, there's little to do in this mausoleum. . . . They're a long while answering." He reached for the bell again impatiently.

"Shall I see you again, Mr. McDonald?"

"I come here, though not as often as my son. No doubt we'll meet." Angus McDonald was offering me his card. I took it, amused.

"Do you think I might need an attorney, Mr. McDonald? I didn't take very seriously what my father said about coming here to claim a heritage."

He frowned at me. "I said I'd advise you, so I will. I think you should take what your father said seriously. I think you should take it very seriously, because there are others who will, even if you don't. As for my card, Miss Craig, I'm not giving it to you to call an attorney. I'm giving it to you so that if you need a *friend*, or possibly two"—he had glanced at his son as he said that, and his frown deepened—"all you need do is reach for the telephone and call this number." He broke off. The door was opening.

I smiled at him involuntarily. "I appreciate what you offer, Mr. McDonald," I said. "Thank you."

The door opened, and a uniformed maid stared out at us curiously. "Dr. McDonald? I thought you'd gone, doctor."

"I brought Miss Craig and my father back," he said. "They met with an accident down in the cutting."

"Miss Craig?"

I hadn't noticed the woman standing behind the maid in deep shadow against the wall because she wore a black dress, and her black hair and dark, expressionless face merged into the shadows there. "Yes?" I said, startled.

"You have red hair," the woman said, moving closer. "I never heard of a Craig with red hair before. The Craigs are all dark-haired, dark-skinned men and women."

"But she is a Craig nevertheless, Mrs. Brunier," the attorney said. "And since she's here to see her uncle, and I with her . . . you'd best take us to him at once!"

He had said it sternly, but she merely stared back at him without moving for a long moment, black eyes glittering in her dark, handsome face before she said quietly, "Her uncle is at the museum with Sandra. It may take a little time. Beth, while I call Mr. Craig, will you take these people through to the reception room?"

"Yes, Mrs. Brunier," the girl said quickly. "Will you come with me, please?"

"You said there had been an accident, doctor? Was anyone hurt?" Mrs. Brunier asked.

Peter stopped. "Luckily not seriously. My father has

a cut head, Miss Craig abrasions. But my father's car is wrecked, and the road's blocked. One of the coal cars ran away downhill and turned over in the cut. It will take a tractor to clear the road."

"Nobody else was involved?"

"We don't know what made the coal car take off the way it did. No doubt Mr. Craig will find that out when he's told."

I walked on with Angus McDonald, leaving Peter talking to the woman. "Who is she, Mr. McDonald?" I asked.

"Mrs. Brunier is your uncle's housekeeper. She's been here since your father's day. Twenty years at least. She's older than she looks. Sometimes I think she's been here too long. She behaves more like a Craig than the Craigs."

"Does her husband work here too?"

"She's a widow," he said shortly. "The reception room is through the next door. Some of your relatives will be in there. Remember the card I gave you. If you find you can't bear it here, get in touch with me, Tracey. I'll try to help you."

He had used my name almost with affection. I looked at him suspiciously, but when our eyes met, I decided that he meant it, so I thanked him.

We were walking into a huge old-fashioned room then, and a group of people sipping coffee in one corner were staring at us curiously. I glanced around, awed by the size of the room and the quality of its furniture. I did not know much about such things, but even I could recognize value and antiquity.

I would have liked to examine everything in this huge, high-ceilinged room piece by piece immediately, but the heavily built man with gray hair sitting with two women in the corner had put down his coffeecup and was standing up to greet us. He reminded me of my father, except that he seemed older, his hair was whiter, and he had a paunch. Like the two women, he studied me with an embarrassing intensity as I approached.

Angus McDonald said harshly "This is Henry Craig's daughter, Tracey, from St. John. Tracey, this is your father's brother Edward Craig; his wife, Mary; and their daughter, Sandra."

"Not Henry's daughter, surely?" my newly found uncle said, staring at me disbelievingly. "A Craig with red hair?" His eyes were not like my father's eyes, I saw now. They were lighter brown, almost amber. Mean eyes. . . .

"She favors her mother, Edward. I thought you'd notice that, since you must remember Elizabeth as well as I do—I'm quite certain your brother John will."

"So that's what you're up to, McDonald?" Edward Craig said angrily.

I glanced from Mr. McDonald to my uncle uneasily. "Mrs. Brunier said something about none of the Craigs having red hair, but I notice your daughter has red hair too. I can't help my coloring; I was born with it. How d'you do, Uncle Edward?"

He shook his head, but he managed to smile. He touched my shoulders with his hands and my cheek with his lips. He smelled too strongly of aftershave, and there was the odor of bourbon on his lips. His daughter got up too. She gave me her hand and a quick peck that seemed spontaneous.

"Hi!" she said, smiling at me. "At least you're my age, and except for the maids, there's been nobody around like that for a long time. Maybe we can get together?"

I knew what it was to be lonely. "Why not, Sandra?" I said. Her mother hadn't moved to greet me, so I went to her and kissed her lightly, feeling her instinctive withdrawal from the touch of my lips.

She stared at me resentfully. "So you're Henry's daughter? I can't see the slightest resemblance. Can you, Edward?"

"Not the slightest," he said quickly.

I was containing anger as I sought a retort to what seemed to me an insult so recently after my father's death, when Angus McDonald came harshly to my defense.

"I can assure you, Ted," he said coldly, "that you're wrong about that, quite wrong. Except for the red hair and green eyes of her mother, Elizabeth, the Craig resemblance *is* there. Look at her and Sandra together if you can't believe me. If I didn't know Sandra has black hair beneath that wig, I could think them sisters, and so could you or anyone else. But Tracey has another Craig characteristic I've discovered during the past few days. In a much greater degree than her father had, *or* any of you have. She has the Craig stubbornness, I guarantee you that. This girl has more obstinacy than her Uncle John has. I'd remember that, if I were you."

There seemed undercurrents here that I couldn't understand. But at least, Angus McDonald was no yesman to the Craigs—that was certain. And as for his son Peter . . .

He was coming in, and behind him cups jingled on a wheeled trolley. A percolator of coffee smelled strong, just the way I needed it. Our eyes met, and he smiled at me across the room. My Uncle Edward had noticed Peter's smile and was considering it as though he had discovered something important, though what it could be, I had no idea.

Peter said, "I told Mrs. Brunier you both needed

coffee after your experience. Did you hear what happened, Mr. Craig?"

Edward Craig was studying Peter with the same dislike he showed his father. He shook his head. "Did something happen? I've been in here with the ladies all afternoon."

Angus McDonald frowned suddenly and asked, "Donald and Ralph with you, Ted?"

For a moment I thought he was going to say yes; then Uncle Edward shook his head. "The boys went to Aberfeld just after lunch. So far as I know, they're still there. It's a wonder you didn't see Ralph's car as you drove through town. He always parks in the main street."

"I didn't see it."

"Then they drove on to Sydney," their mother said. "Ralph said they might do that, I noticed the bandage on your head when you came in, Mr. McDonald. And the girl's frock is dirty and torn. Did you have an accident, then? Is that why your son came back with you?"

My Aunt Mary was smarter than her husband, I decided, and much more observant.

Angus McDonald said bluntly, "One of the coal cars ran down the hill from the old marshaling yards and collided with us as we left the cutting. A few seconds quicker, and we'd both be dead." He took a cup of coffee from the maid and added, "We can both use this. It was too close to be pleasant."

My Uncle Edward sat down again and picked up his cup, but his wife was staring at us disbelievingly. "I can't understand how that could happen."

"Neither can I, Mrs. Craig!" Angus McDonald said. "But I'm working at it, you can be sure of that. And here comes John Craig, who will be as keen to find the answer as I am."

They all glanced at the door, and I with them, full of curiosity to see the man who had relented enough to have me brought here, yet hated my father for some wrong, real or imaginary. I couldn't think of that any other way, despite my father's admission in the letter of instruction that Mr. McDonald had brought me.

At first, all I saw of John Craig as he walked in was that he stood six feet tall and looked younger than his sixty years. He wore casual clothes as untidily as my father, and there was a resemblance, although John Craig was not as handsome as Dad.

"So this is the girl?" he said gruffly, staring at me.

I saw his eyes clearly for the first time then. Eyes almost as amber as Edward's, though less mean, eyes full of dark brown flecks. Eyes, I saw at once, that were prepared to dislike me.

"I'm Tracey Craig, sir," I said defiantly.

"That I can see," he said unpleasantly. "Even if your father hadn't told me things he wanted me to know about you." His expression changed subtly, though, as he examined me. I had the impression that suddenly he had to force himself to dislike me. He said reluctantly, "He was right in one thing. You're like your mother for looks."

"Am I?" I said stiffly. "I wouldn't know. My mother died when I was born." I hesitated. "I never saw a portrait of her."

"You'll find none in this house either," he said dryly, and turned from me abruptly to Angus McDonald. "All finished in St. John, and left neat and tidy?"

"I did what you asked of me," Angus McDonald said. "No more, no less."

My uncle nodded. "Good. Arrange an allowance for her. She is to get the same as the others; and like the others, she'll have to earn it while I control Craig

Investments. Now, what's this about an accident you had coming in? Yvonne said something about a runaway coal car from old yards." Talking to Angus McDonald, he had pressed the bell near where the maid waited with the coffee. Mrs. Brunier came in so quickly that it occurred to me she had been listening outside the door, but that thought seemed foolish even as I thought it.

"Yes?"

"Yvonne, do you have a room ready for her?"

"Yes."

It did not seem to interest him enough to ask her where, or which one, I noticed. He merely nodded uninterestedly. "When she's ready, show Miss Craig to her room and see she's made comfortable there. No doubt she'll want to clean up before dinner. Her frock is torn."

I remembered suddenly that everything I possessed was still in Angus McDonald's car. I said, dismayed, "I don't have any clothes!"

He studied me, frowning. "You have nothing?"

Angus McDonald said for me, "Her clothes are in the automobile trunk. It will take an iron bar to prize it open. What happened down there was worse than you all seem to think. I'd like to discuss that and several other things with you before I leave, John. And I have a wife waiting for me in Aberfeld, I'll have you know."

John Craig smiled unexpectedly. "Come with me to my study, then, Angus. We can talk there. Peter, I'll send him home if you've calls to make! Yvonne, bring us coffee, and something to give it flavor." He looked at me, the smile still lingering faintly. "I'll send two of the gardeners down in the jeep to prize out your belongings."

"Thank you." I thought if he ever unbent enough

to smile at me the way he had at Angus McDonald, I could like him. Smiling, he looked like my father.

Peter McDonald said quietly, "Not too much flavoring in that coffee, Yvonne."

She nodded. "I understand, Dr. McDonald."

I discovered Peter McDonald watching me, smiling.

"Oh, come on," he said. "It shouldn't make you feel that miserable, Tracey. Walk to the door with me. I have patients to think about, so I must go. You can admire the lawns from the front door—they're your uncle's pride and joy. There's never a leaf out of place till winter comes." He looked at the others. "Good day, Mr. Craig, ladies."

Sandra gave him a pleasant good-bye; her parents merely nodded surlily.

In the great wide passage I said, "But I don't like chess."

He chuckled. "Uncle John's landscaping affects you that way, does it? Don't you play chess?"

"Dad played chess, but I just wasn't interested. Why?"

"A pity," he said. "It might have helped you at Glamis. Your Uncle John loves the game. But he rarely finds anyone to play with." We had reached the great front doors, and he opened them and looked out. "There goes the jeep, You should have your things soon now. I tried to open the trunk while we were down there, but it's jammed fast."

The door faced the gates. I could see the cutting, the smashed automobile, and the overturned coal car. I shivered involuntarily and found him studying me sympathetically, his handsome face grim.

"I just don't want to think about it," I said.

"Nobody was hurt, Tracey—and an accident like that one shouldn't happen again."

"Peter," I said obstinately, "I saw someone pushing

it, and I saw someone opening the points, if that's what the lever he pulled does. It may not have been meant to hurt anyone, but it was no accident that it moved. Or came down the hill."

"Could you recognize the man?" he asked me, frowning. "Could you give a description of him, if you had to?"

"Of course not. He was too far away. Look, there's a car coming up the hill now. Could you describe the people in it? It's on the other road, but it's about level with the cutting."

He chuckled. "I could describe them exactly, Tracey, because I recognize the car. It belongs to your cousin, Ralph, who's driving. The passenger is his brother, Donald. You've given me a thought, though. If there *was* someone as you said, and he came from anywhere within twenty miles of here, he'd recognize Dad's car."

"He wouldn't know me?"

"No. But suppose he lived here and knew when Dad was bringing you here?" He frowned suddenly. "Tracey, suppose someone aimed that thing at the car? Knowing my father was bringing you to Glamis today. Because if it was not an accident, have to think of it as something far more serious. Something some person unknown planned against your coming."

I shook my head. "I can't believe they'd want to *kill* us," I said.

"*You*," he said. "Not the plural. Just you. Neither can I believe it, Tracey. But I *can* think of a motive. Greed."

I stared at him, appalled. "Greed? But I don't have *anything*!" I protested, frightened suddenly.

"True," he said. "But you are a Craig, and your Uncle John, who has control of the Craig wealth, has accepted you back into the family. Which makes you one of his heirs, and that much less for someone else who did not expect this to happen. Someone who might want to prevent it if possible."

"I don't want their money! I'll tell them so!" I watched a car pull in to the foot of the steps and stop behind Peter's car. Two men were climbing stiffly from a powerful sports car, both young, dark-haired men.

"Be careful, Tracey," he said in a low voice. "That's all. Dad gave you our phone number. If anything frightens you here or seems to threaten you, *use* it. If Dad doesn't answer, I will. If we had to, we'd take you away from Glamis. I promise you that."

"But . . ."

"Just don't forget what I said," he muttered warningly. He turned, grinning. "Here come two cousins you haven't met. Ralph and Donald Craig."

I said hello to them, my mind still on the frightening things Peter had been saying. I studied them with suspicion. Ralph Craig was a sturdy man of about thirty; he had the family resemblance, but his eyes were a soft, dark brown. He seemed just a nice young man, trying to be polite to a girl cousin he was meeting for the first time. Donald was five years younger, a different type, slim for a Craig, and shorter, his eyes devoid of any warmth even when he was saying pleasant things to me.

"Mrs. Brunier is going upstairs now, Miss Craig."

There was relief in the appearance of the maid. I thanked her and said I'd come right away. Peter gave me an encouraging smile and went down the steps looking at his watch as though he had remembered a patient. I walked back to the stairs with the two men to where Mrs. Brunier waited. It occurred to me that I had been looking at them both in the light of my newly found suspicion, which seemed hardly fair, since they had just returned to Glamis.

"Have you come from Aberfeld?" I asked Ralph politely.

"From Sydney," he said. "I had business there for Uncle John. Donald—"

"Donald has only one thing in mind," his brother interrupted him. "To wash away the dust. Why my brother drives an open sports car, I'll never know, Tracey. But don't ever let him persuade you to ride in it with him."

"Why not?" I asked. "It looks terrific."

"Oh it *is*. But for a guy who does everything else in less than moderation, old Ralph changes to a demon when he gets behind the wheel of a sports car. He drives like a maniac! That's why I need a drink now. He scares the daylights out of me. My nerves are all shot."

"Really, Donald . . . !" his brother began to protest.

Donald shook his head. "One of these days you're going to kill yourself with that heap, Ralph. I don't want to be your passenger when you do." We had reached the foot of the stairs and he stopped and studied me intently with those expressionless eyes. "We usually have a quiet family drink in the reception room before dinner, Tracey. Don't miss it. Today's session should be interesting, with a new cousin in the house."

"I don't drink much," I admitted. "Punch at birthday parties, and a light wine with special-occasion dinners."

"And you a *Craig*?" His eyes studied me briefly. "We'll do something about that, Ralph!"

"If she doesn't want to drink, why should she?" Ralph said. "This family drinks far too much, except for Uncle John and me."

"Whose side are you on?" his brother jeered. "When

you come down, Tracey, I'll mix you one of my special cocktails. It's as gentle as a malted, liquorwise, and a treat for even the taste buds of naïve young girls like you."

I felt myself flush angrily, but I merely said, "Really?"

As I turned away from them and followed Mrs. Brunier upstairs, I heard Ralph murmur, "You shouldn't say things like that, Donald. *I* don't think she's naïve."

"If she wasn't, would she *be* here?" his brother retorted.

My door was on the second floor at the end of a passage leading away from the stairs. I stared around curiously as Mrs. Brunier opened the door for me. It was not just a bedroom, as I had expected. It was a suite as large as our St. John apartment. There was an open fireplace in the huge bedroom, and an old-fashioned bed that looked as though it could sleep half a dozen, and more clothes closets than I could possibly use.

"We use coal fires through late fall and winter," Mrs. Brunier said. "One of the maids will light yours each evening in time to warm the room for the night for you. It's best you leave the fire alone if you're not used to coal fires."

"I'm not, Mrs. Brunier," I admitted. "We had central heating at St. John."

"Here we prefer coal," she said. "From our mines. There's nothing can compare with a glowing coal fire in winter, when there's snow and ice outside."

I noticed the way Mrs. Brunier said "our" mines. As though she identified herself with the Craig family. I could understand that happening when someone worked closely with a family as she must have done for years at Glamis. I studied her covertly. In the hall

I had thought her a handsome woman even with that stern expression. But under the chandelier in my bedroom I could see that she was more than that. Yvonne Brunier was still a beautiful woman, with those large, slanted brown eyes and the full but shapely lips that some French women have. Hers were the classic features of beautiful European women descended from the old aristocracy, but made more earthy, I suspected, from some healthier infusion of more common blood. Beneath the plain black dress that had only white lace at throat and breast to relieve it, I could glimpse a round-breasted voluptuous figure that even her uniform-like clothing couldn't possibly hide.

It occurred to me that with makeup on, her black hair brushed up into some mod style, and dressed for some occasion, Yvonne Brunier would be sensational. It seemed a wonder to me that my Uncle John, who was still a bachelor and presentable even at sixty, hadn't noticed Yvonne's possibilities. After all, they'd been together here for twenty years.

I smiled secretly. Perhaps he had. Despite the air of authority he wore like protective medieval armor, Uncle John seemed both male and human to me.

"Your bell is beside your bed, Miss Craig," Yvonne Brunier was saying. "Beth will answer if you ring. She's running your bath, and will lay out whatever clothes you need when they arrive, if you tell her what you intend to wear."

I shook my head. "I'm used to doing things like that for myself, Mrs. Brunier," I said. "I think I'd prefer it that way. There must be something more useful Beth could be doing?"

She gave me an appraising glance. "There *is*, Miss Craig, but I was instructed to make you comfortable moving in here, and that's what I'm doing. I wish some of the others thought as you do. But on the other hand, we don't encourage laziness in *anyone* at Glamis. People are asked to remember that before they ring the bell for a maid. It takes time for a girl to leave whatever she's doing and come up here, or to the floors above."

"I'll remember that if I'm ever tempted to use the bell." I smiled. "But I can't think of anything I'd be remotely likely to want a maid to do for me. Other than attending to lighting the coal fire you mentioned. I wouldn't have any clues there."

She mellowed perceptibly. "Beth looks after this floor. She will bring you morning coffee when she serves the others before breakfast, whether you ring or not. Your rooms will be cleaned each morning while you are downstairs, your used clothes and linen taken away for laundering. Would you like to see the rest of your suite now, before I leave?"

I followed her into a second room, furnished as a study. It had deep chairs and an old-fashioned rolltop cedar desk. There was a comfortably upholstered sofa where a girl could put her feet up when tired.

"The library is downstairs," she said. "You may bring books from it to your rooms whenever you wish, and there are always late-issue magazines on the library racks. You can relax and read in comfort in here."

"I like these rooms!" I said involuntarily. "It's like having your own apartment."

"You can have privacy here, Miss Craig," she said. "We all need that at times. Your bathroom plumbing is modern; the bathroom was completely remodeled a few months ago."

She waited near the study door to show it to me, but curiosity had drawn me to the window to stare out. My windows looked down across the lawns to the building adjoining the wall that I had noticed as we drove in. Beyond the wall was the sea and a glimpse of receding headlands made vague by distance.

I stared across at the building curiously. "What place is that under the wall?"

"The museum."

I frowned. "A museum of what, Mrs. Brunier?"

"Of medieval things Mr. Craig collected from Europe. Your uncle is a famous antiquarian and collector. The museum is his hobby. Some of the pieces in there are priceless—particularly in the downstairs chambers."

"Really?" I said eagerly. "Do you think he'd let me *see* them?"

She smiled faintly at my enthusiasm, giving me the impression that she did not share it. "It wouldn't surprise me if he put you to work among them," she said. "If he finds out you are interested in such things. Sandra has been helping him with cataloging, but she has no interest in the work whatsoever. Ralph is the only Craig who helps him with museum work. Ralph is learning to restore fragile artifacts, some very old."

"But I'd like that," I said quickly. "I mean . . . working with things like that is something I've always wanted to do. I took archaeology at college last year." I came across the room to her impetuously. "Mrs. Brunier, do you suppose if I asked Uncle John, he'd let me work in there? He told Mr. McDonald he expected me to earn my allowance as everyone else at Glamis has to earn theirs."

She took a step away from me as I reached her, as though she thought I might touch her and was afraid of the contact. She studied my face for a long moment before she replied.

"I'm not sure," she said slowly. "Perhaps he would. Perhaps not. It would mean seeing you there where he spends most of his time. . . . There are undercurrents here at Glamis that you do not seem to realize exist. Things that have their roots in a past that happened before you were born. But if this work is something you want, perhaps I could help you."

"Mrs. Brunier, if only you would!"

"Very well," she said. "But don't go to him about it, Miss Craig. If you do that, you will only antagonize others more. I will tell him what you said—he listens to me. I think after he has thought about it, he may ask you to work there. If he can find it in his heart to bear you near him."

I stared at her, shocked by what she had said, hearing the maid Beth running water hard in my bathroom, smelling something fragrant and refreshing she was adding to my bath.

"What do you mean, Mrs. Brunier?" I asked her. "To *bear* me near him? I'm no leper!"

"He loved your mother," she said quietly. "That was why he never married. And as I remember her, Elizabeth lives again in you, Miss Craig. Come, I'll show you the bathroom."

I followed her silently. I was remembering suddenly what my father had written when he ordered me to come to Glamis: "I have never spoken to you of my family, or of my brother John. Years ago I did something that my family believed wronged John deeply, and the Craigs are a dour people who never forgive a wrong. . . ."

Chapter *FOUR*

I was beginning to think Uncle John had been joking when he said that his relatives at Glamis must earn their allowance. At breakfast Uncle John had eaten hastily, and ordered the chauffeur to wait for him at the entrance. Immediately afterward he went speeding off to the mines for a conference.

When he was leaving, he looked at me as though about to say something other than the curt good-bye he had given us collectively, and I thought eagerly of Mrs. Brunier's promise, imagining myself as good as at work in the museum. But he scowled suddenly as though he had had second thoughts about whatever it was he had been going to say to me. He nodded and went to his study down the passage for his briefcase. He passed by the breakfast-room door on his way back and drove away.

Uncle John, it seemed to me, earned *his* allowance, if he had one, but that seemed more than I could say for the others. Mrs. Craig went back to her room after telling Sandra that she was exhausted and hadn't slept well last night. Her husband followed her after choosing a sporting magazine from the library. Donald gave Mrs. Brunier instructions to have his car brought around to the front steps because he had a business appointment in Aberfeld. But when the car was brought and Donald went out to it, from the window I noticed that it was golf clubs he carried, not a briefcase, and he wore casual clothes instead of the business suit I expected.

I lingered after Donald had gone, talking to Sandra, with Ralph listening silently, and neither of them seemed in any hurry to go to work in the museum if they *were* working there this morning.

I had been talking to Sandra about college life in St. John when Ralph became suddenly interested and asked me what subjects I'd been studying in my arts course. He scowled when I told him.

"Archaeology and medieval history?" he said, staring at me. "Why?"

"They were only part of the course."

"I know that," he said angrily. "So your father remembered where Uncle John's interest lay? That's obvious. I suppose he knew about the museum too, even though it wasn't until after he left Glamis that Uncle John started searching for artifacts in Europe and the Middle East."

He sounded so resentful that I stared at him in dismay. "I'm not sure that I know what you mean," I said. "I didn't know that I had an Uncle John, or any other relative than my father, when I enrolled in the faculty. That was more than a year ago. I didn't even know Glamis existed!"

His brown eyes avoided my indignant ones uneasily. "I didn't say you did, Tracey," he muttered. "But your father influenced you to take those subjects. We know why. Because he expected that to help establish you here. To influence Uncle John in your favor."

"Ralph doesn't mean that we blame you for it, Tracey," his sister said with a warning glance at him. "We're not like the others. We want to accept you."

"I'll buy that, Tracey," her brother said, his smile malicious. "If you can tell us why you chose to study subjects most girls avoid?"

"I chose them as part of my study program because they happen to be subjects I am interested in," I retorted angrily. "Dad had a lot of books on both subjects, and I read all he had on both archaeology and medieval history. My father had nothing to do with my choice of them. I knew if I took them as part of my studies for a degree they'd help me get it. And they would have. I got honors in both subjects for last year's work."

"Your father *just happened* to have the right books?" he said cynically.

"Maybe. They were there, so I read them. And I found that what they contained interested me, so I retained a lot of it in my memory. That helped me last year. It would have again this year, only . . ." I broke off.

"Only your father died," he said. "Okay, little naïve girl. Why did you ask Mrs. Brunier to try to get you into the museum to work with Uncle John? Tell me that."

Sandra glared at me suddenly. "She *didn't!*"

"She *did*," Ralph said. "She's after your job, Sandra."

"Did Mrs. Brunier tell you that?" I demanded fiercely.

"Mrs. Brunier didn't tell me anything," he said. "You were overheard saying it. And my informant was telling the truth. You happen to be one of those people who get red faces when they're caught out in something underhand. You're flushing right up to the roots of your hair right now, cousin."

It was that wretched maid—what was her name, Beth? It had to be. And even though it wasn't really deserved, the realization was making my face hotter. I wanted to run away from them both, even though Sandra was looking at him as though she still couldn't quite believe what he said.

"Well?" Ralph's look was slyly triumphant.

I wondered why I had ever thought *him* a nice man! "Look!" I said, "I don't want Sandra's job, and I never said I did. But if I have to work here, I'd sooner it was in the museum. *If* I stay here."

"I'll bet," he said. "Because Uncle John is there—"

"That's enough, Ralph!" Sandra said unexpectedly. "Leave her alone."

"Why should I?" he demanded, glaring at her, "What d'you think Donald would do if he were here? She's the way Dad said her father was. You can't trust her, Sandra." He glanced at me angrily. "And to think we argued against Donald and the others that she should come to Glamis. It's happening just the way they said it would. She's accepted by Uncle John, she's given a home here and an allowance. The next thing you know, she'll be working with him in the museum instead of you."

"I've never liked working in that gruesome tomb anyhow!" Sandra said tartly, glancing at me. "I'm not like you. Dead things frighten me. But it just might be bearable if I had another girl working with me on cataloging."

"You'd better not let Donald hear you suggest *that*!" Ralph said grimly. "*Excuse* me!" He got up, frowning.

"Donald doesn't frighten me," his sister said. She shook her head nervously, as though she shuddered. "But Ivan *does*. He's always spying on someone. It was Ivan who told you what Tracey said wasn't it?"

"Why don't you find that out for yourself?" her brother growled. "He's waiting for us over there. Did I tell you I saw a light in the museum again last night? Uncle John was in his study, and I have the only other key. When I told him, he said I was imagining things.

He came in here with me, and we looked across, but the light was gone."

"So Uncle John was right, you did imagine it."

"And maybe that imbecile Ivan has his own way in," her brother said disgustedly.

"Why are you so sure it's Ivan?" She glanced uneasily at the open window, as though she expected an eavesdropper.

He scowled at her. "Why? Because there's nothing ever out of place. Nothing ever *stolen*. It has to be Ivan. Why do you think Uncle John never worries when I tell him about the light? I believe he *knows* damned well who the prowler is. Otherwise he'd have all the police on Cape Breton Island here within the hour. You know how he values the artifacts. Insurance could never replace them." He hesitated and glanced at me, frowning. "Look, Tracey—maybe what you said to Yvonne Brunier was said innocently because you are interested in junk like that in the museum. But consider how all this—your coming here and Uncle John's change of heart about you—must seem to *us*."

Still angry, I said coldly, "How *does* it seem to you, cousin?"

"It seems unfair, to say the least of it!" he said indignantly. "Because of your father, the whole of the Craig estates were left to Uncle John, instead of being divided equally among the surviving descendants when our grandparents died, as had always happened before in the Craig family. The rest of us have had to subsist here like poor relations ever since, and not much consolation to us that your father and you were left even worse off than we were."

"Much worse off," I said sarcastically, glancing around. "But surely you can't blame *me* for what happened? I had nothing to do with that!"

"I argued that in your favor," he said. "And Sandra

went along with it. We were the only ones who thought so, when Uncle John told us your father had written asking him to take you. But now that you're here and accepted by him, who's to say Uncle John won't do what his father did and leave the whole estate to the one *he* prefers? Or that the sole heir might not prove to be you?"

"*Me?*" I stared at him, startled. "But that's impossible! Why should he? He hated Dad, and he's shown no sign of liking me."

He glanced at Sandra, then back at me, frowning. "Tracey, do you know what happened here that started all this? Be honest, Tracey—do you?"

"Until yesterday I didn't. I'd swear to that. But yesterday Mrs. Brunier said that Uncle John . . . was in love with my mother." He started to interrupt, but I stopped him. "No, wait, Ralph! She only used it as an argument against my working in the museum. Did Beth tell you that?"

"Beth?" he said in a surprised voice. "Why *Beth?*"

"She was in the bathroom when we were talking. She could've heard."

He shook his head. "It wasn't Beth, Tracey. And don't try to make me tell you who it was. Sometimes it's useful to have a source of information in a place like Glamis. Didn't Macbeth have his witches?"

"They destroyed him," I said.

He smiled without mirth. "I'm no Macbeth," he said grimly. "I don't have his ambition, or his greed to take all. How did *your* particular witch use Uncle John's love life as an argument against you working in the museum?"

"She said she'd mention to Uncle John that I would like to work in the museum. But she said she doubted that he could bear me near him, and he spent a lot of time in there—"

"He spends every moment in the museum he can spare from multiplying the Craig money. You can say that again," he interrupted me. "But go on."

"She made me angry saying that. I asked her did she think I was a leper? And she said . . ." I hesitated, seeing her remarks in a different, a more sinister way, after some of the things Ralph Craig had been saying. "She said that Uncle John was in love with my mother, and that was why he never married. And she said that . . . that my mother lives again in me."

He stared at me, frowning. "Both Dad and Mother said that too. That they were shocked by the resemblance to your mother when you came in with Angus McDonald yesterday."

"Mother said the likeness was positively weird," Sandra said. "She said it could have *been* your mother walking into the reception room the way she was at your age before your father took her away from Uncle John."

I scowled at Sandra. "My mother had the right to choose the man she wanted to marry, Sandra. You know that. You're a woman. It wasn't the Middle Ages when all this happened. It had to be about 1950 or 1951. The Craig family had no right whatever to decide who she'd marry. Just because Uncle John was in love with my mother doesn't mean she was in love with him. She chose Dad, and to me that means she loved him. And I don't blame her for the choice, either. Dad seems to me to have been a better choice for a husband than Uncle John could ever be, even with all the wealth you say he has."

"Then she should have decided that in the first place," Ralph said vindictively. "Before she married Uncle John."

I stared at him uncomprehendingly, a part of my

mind refusing to believe what he had said. "Before she . . . *what*?"

He looked away. "I'm sorry I said that, Tracey. It wasn't meant to hurt you. But how can I be sure that all this ignorance of yours isn't just pretense?"

"Is this the truth?" I felt sick suddenly, thinking about it. Yet it seemed to me that it had to be the truth. It explained the bitterness here that I had thought merely stupid prejudice.

"We've always known what happened, Tracey," Sandra said. "Uncle John met your mother in Montreal, where they were at college together. They became engaged there, and the day he graduated, they were married. He brought her to Glamis, and they were married in Aberfeld. Uncle John was the eldest son, so Grandfather Craig gave him the management of the estate. Uncle John created Craig Investments, and everything began to expand and prosper incredibly almost at once. Except Uncle John's marriage. He was away too much on corporation business. Montreal, Quebec, then Europe, South America, the Far East. When he came back from London a year after they married, your mother told him she'd fallen in love with your father and was leaving him."

"She couldn't *do* that!" But how did I know that? I wondered. "I never knew my mother. My father spoke of her only when, prompted by the questions asked of me by curious friends, I felt impelled to find answers. But nothing like this had ever occurred to me."

"Nobody is asking you to believe us," Ralph said. "No doubt Angus McDonald has the divorce recorded in his office."

"There was a *divorce*?" I muttered sickly.

"With your father named as corespondent, Tracey," Sandra said quietly. "Dad said they kept it as quiet as possible, and the case was not contested."

"Uncle John had no difficulty getting the divorce, though," Ralph Craig said. "Your mother was divorced on grounds of adultery. She went off to St. John with your father, and as soon as possible, they were married there."

Cold sweat started on my forehead as I listened. I began to feel sick.

"Oh, come on, Ralph," his sister said, getting up. "Or Ivan will go off someplace, and we'll both catch hell from Uncle John when he finds Ivan has done nothing. We're supposed to have those cases unpacked and checked for any damage. Remember?"

"Is she all right?" her brother's voice said anxiously. "She looks pretty sick about it. But all I told her was the truth, and easily proven."

"Just leave her alone," Sandra said curtly. "Can't you!"

"Okay, okay!" he said. "But she looks sick to me."

I heard him walk away while I fought the threat of tears.

I heard him go out, and Sandra's voice asked me anxiously, "Are you okay, Tracey?"

"Oh, I'm fine," I said bitterly. "What do you expect from a girl who's just been told her mother was an adulteress?"

"I'm sorry Ralph said those things to you, Tracey," she said nervously. "Men are so tactless. But he didn't say it to hurt you, and it *is* the truth. Donald might say things deliberately to hurt people, Donald can be cruel like that, but not Ralph."

"So I know what happened now," I said, fighting tears. "I don't like it, but I *know*! Do you want me to *thank* your brother for that?"

She shook her head, studying my face, her large gray eyes moist with sympathy suddenly, so that I remembered how young she was, and that I had been prepared to like her yesterday.

"Tracey," she said uncertainly, "try not to feel too badly about it. Even here on Cape Breton Island we hear about divorces happening among people we know. Not every marriage can be a good one. And sometimes it must be better to cut your losses and start again. So people who have made a mistake break up and remarry. Let me walk up to your room with you. You look positively ill."

I didn't want her help, even though the sympathy in her voice was making me cry now. "Can't you just . . . leave me alone?" I muttered savagely.

"For a little while I thought you and I might have become friends," she said sadly. "But if that's the way you want it . . .?"

I had hoped that too, I realized vaguely, but Ralph Craig had made me feel that all I wanted was to escape from her at any cost. At that moment I hated the Craigs of Glamis, *all* of them. Even Uncle John Craig, the innocent party in what had happened.

I stared at her angrily through tears. "Friends? A friend at Glamis, when I know you all hate me?"

"That's just not true, Tracey!" she stammered, taking a step back from my angry approach.

"And I know *why* you hate me," I stormed, using rage to stem my tears. "It's because you're horrid greedy people! Your brother talked about you subsisting at Glamis like poor relations! You're here for just one reason, all of you. You know Uncle John's health is failing, and your only interest is in the division of the estate after his death. That's why you're here, and that's what you're waiting for. And wild horses couldn't drag *one of you* away from Glamis until that happens."

"No!" I saw fear of me in her eyes suddenly. "No, you're wrong, Tracey! *Please* listen to me!"

"I listened to your brother," I reminded her bitterly. "Now, you listen to me, Sandra! Coming here, I had no thought of any inheritance. I doubt that I'd have accepted it if there had been one waiting here for me to take—knowing that you hated my father. But I'm beginning to change my mind about that. And I'm a Craig too, so you aren't going to embarrass me into leaving, and you can't frighten me away as maybe someone tried to do yesterday!"

Her eyes widened abruptly in a face suddenly pale. "You can't think one of *us* had anything to do with your accident?"

"Accident?" I scoffed furiously. "Maybe we should let the *police* decide that, Sandra."

It was a foolish thing to say, I thought, but I savored her shock and dismay for a long moment while she stared at me wide-eyed, trying to find a reply. She found then that she had none, and turned and ran from the room. Mrs. Brunier, coming in, followed by one of the maids, stepped aside hastily and looked after her in surprise. Our eyes met as Mrs. Brunier came in, and she shook her head slightly, her usually full lips drawn tighter than usual in disapproval. Brown eyes studied me, no doubt noticing the signs of recent tears and more recent anger that I couldn't hide.

"Will you be going out this morning, Miss Craig?" she asked me, as though prepared to organize the morning usefully for me.

I shook my head. "I thought I'd walk in the grounds if there's nothing useful I can do in the house. Is there, Mrs. Brunier?"

She smiled faintly. "The family never does housework, Miss Craig. We have servants to do that." She glanced at the maid gathering the dishes, and lowered her voice. "I mentioned the matter we discussed to Mr. Craig. Did he say anything to you about museum work?"

"No, Mrs. Brunier. I had the impression he was going to say something as he was leaving, but he seemed to change his mind."

She nodded. "It was a very important conference he had. It involves an export contract for coal worth several million dollars. He had too much on his mind this morning to make any decisions about you. But no doubt he will discuss it with you on his return. Meantime, I wouldn't talk about it to other members of the family if I were you, Miss Craig. They may be tempted to try to prevent it. Once he makes a decision, they know they can't make him change his mind, so they don't try."

I shrugged. "It's too late for that, Mrs. Brunier. We were overheard discussing it yesterday, and whoever heard told Ralph."

She frowned, her dark eyes malevolent suddenly. "*Beth* was in your rooms! I thought she knew better than that. I'll speak to her in my office later!" She studied me briefly, still angry. "It was *this* you were discussing in here?"

I nodded. "I was angry at that, and at other things Ralph said."

She nodded. "I don't blame you. But that stupid girl won't do anything like that again. I'll see to that."

"It wasn't the maid," I said, remembering. "I thought that too. But Ralph said the person who told him was called Ivan."

"*Ivan*?"

I would have doubted that anything I could say could possibly upset Yvonne Brunier's studied calm, but that had. She had paled to the lips, and I could see fear in her dark eyes quite plainly.

"Is something the matter, Mrs. Brunier?" I asked anxiously.

She shook her head. "What else did he say about Ivan?"

"Nothing else." I thought back. Almost in the same context, Ralph Craig had talked about mysterious lights in the museum at night, and had hinted Uncle John knew who the prowler was. But he hadn't openly connected Ivan with that, whoever Ivan was. I decided against mentioning the lights. "Who is Ivan, Mrs. Brunier?"

Her eyes avoided mine, as though she thought I might learn too much about her and betray her.

She hesitated before replying in a low voice. "Ivan is my son. He was born here in Glamis. He was a retarded child, but your uncle sent him to the best doctors in Canada so that he can live a normal life now. He works in the museum. You'll meet him there, no doubt."

I nodded, not knowing what to say, except, "Then please don't blame Ivan for telling Ralph what he overheard. Ivan must've been in the passage. The door was open, remember? And no doubt he just mentioned it innocently to Ralph because they work together in the museum."

"It caused you distress," she said grimly. "So he will be punished for that. He won't repeat anything he overhears to Ralph Craig again, or to any of the others, believe me."

"It wasn't Ivan who caused me distress," I said. "Please, can't we just forget it? I've nothing against your son. I'm not angry about something he could not have known would hurt me. How can I be angry with him?"

"Very well, Miss Craig," she said. "I will speak to

him, because it must not happen again—but he will not be punished."

"Thank you, Mrs. Brunier," I said, smiling slightly. "I think I'll go for a walk in the sunshine, while there is still fall sunshine here."

She studied me thoughtfully. "Be careful to keep away from the old mine shafts. They have been covered, but they can be dangerous."

"I'll be careful," Mrs. Brunier."

"I wasn't sure what to expect when they told me you were coming here, Miss Craig," she said. "But you are different from the others. It is true that you resemble your mother, but your nature is not hers. You are more like your Uncle John than any other Craig I have ever known."

I thought of what she had said as I went up to my room and changed into slacks and strong shoes for better walking. Coming from the housekeeper, any favorable comparison of me with Uncle John had to be a compliment. She was wrong, of course. All my friends thought me like Dad. Maybe I should feel flattered, though? Because it seemed obvious that Uncle John was Yvonne Brunier's pinup.

Perhaps it was only something born of his kindness to her retarded son, but from the way she spoke of him, and the way she identified herself with the things he did, I was beginning to suspect that in her own calm way Yvonne Brunier was in love with my Uncle John.

I remembered too that none of the others had seemed to know the facts of today's big coal deal the way she did. And then there was the way she had been so sure he would listen to her when she told him of my interest in museum work.

Thinking of these things as I came downstairs, I

found myself turning automatically away from Glamis. I walked instead toward the entrance gates and the old railroad marshaling yard with its dilapidated and long-unused rolling stock.

Chapter FIVE

Uncle John had an orderly mind, I decided as I walked past a row of pawns bordering one end of his lawns. So he'd probably have something to say to me about the museum sooner or later. A man like Uncle John was unlikely to forget anything brought to his attention until he had dealt with it one way or the other. I decided Yvonne Brunier could prove to be a good ally if I ever needed one at Glamis. Only now I wasn't sure that I wanted to work in the museum with Ralph Craig or his sister.

Sheltered by the walls of Glamis, I was surprised when I walked through the open gates and met the bite of the wind. My walk was suddenly less pleasant than it had been on the other side of the great stone wall looming above me. I shivered, staring around, and not entirely from the chill of wind coming in from a cold green sea. The red road winding up from the roofs of Aberfeld reminded me of my terror just before arriving here. It seemed much longer than yesterday that, still shaken from the collision, I had ridden up here with Peter McDonald. It was refreshing to think of him, though, even if he hadn't kept his promise to visit me as a patient this morning when he came to see Uncle John.

Perhaps Uncle John had phoned him not to come because he would be away at his silly conference, but that was no excuse for Peter not calling to see *me*. My bruises were still painful, my muscles stiff. I had needed a doctor, and it was straining the doctor-patient relationship that he hadn't come. Or so I told myself. But standing under the wall reminded me again of yesterday, and thoughts of Peter McDonald's dark, handsome face faded. Yesterday, everyone, including Peter, had been concerned that I had almost been killed down in that area that now looked empty and harmless in morning sunlight.

But what had any of them done about it? So far as I knew, nothing. Peter's father had almost been killed with me, and hadn't he given me vague warnings of danger at Glamis? Why, he'd even given me his card so that I could phone him if I needed help.

And Peter had gone a step farther than that and talked about whisking me away from Glamis if I felt scared or threatened at any hour of the day or night. And then there was my Uncle John, who had said he would send men to check on what had happened. All his men seemed to have done was clear the road and have Mr. McDonald's poor limousine towed away.

Yet it was all so simple, really, or so it seemed to me, walking toward the rank grass and weeds that sprouted among the rusted cars, some overturned and almost covered by the growth. All anyone had to do was check the car down at the cut, and the points over here where the rusted iron rails of the former railroad yard joined tracks that had once run downhill from the entrance gates of Glamis to Aberfeld. If they had been greased, then my statement was proven that someone had started the car rolling down to the cut, where it had almost killed us.

Not that *I* needed proof. I *knew* what I saw, and what I saw was a man pushing the car toward the junction with the other line, and then hurrying back to throw the switch before it reached there.

The rails were just ahead now. I could see crushed

grass where the speeding car had passed. The rails I
followed began to curve now, for the junction with
what I regarded as the main track. It was here that the
car had almost turned over. The junction must be just
ahead, closer to the road. There had been no track
near the gates of Glamis. It must've been torn up and
removed long ago. But I began to see rails among
shorter grass beside the road on my left now. I stopped
abruptly. Something lay among long grass on my right,
as though thrown there carelessly when someone finished with it.

I had to force my way through long grass to reach
it. I stared down in dismay. It was one thing, I was
learning, to suspect that what had happened had been
deliberate, but it was quite another thing to find your
suspicion crystallize into certainty when you found what
you considered proof. It lay partly hidden in the long
grass, a seven-pound tin that had once held maple
syrup, perhaps for Mrs. Brunier's kitchen. Now it held
a lining of thick black grease. The same kind of grease
soaked a piece of rag bound to what looked like the
end of a broom handle thrust into the can.

The rail junction was twenty yards farther on, but I
knew what I would find when I got there. The mov-
able section of track had smeared thick grease all
over the roadbed, and thrown it in globs upon the
rails of the main track where it merged with the track
from the marshaling yard. The speeding car had burned
or squeezed most of the black grease from the rails
it used, but the evidence was still there. As it must have
been found on the wheels of the overturned car in the
cut, if the men who had salvaged it had looked. As I
was sure now I must find thick grease on the switch
in the marshaling yards.

Among the long grass I had got grease on my shoes
and the legs of my slacks, I discovered disgustedly. I

hoped the maids at Glamis were good at dry cleaning, because I wasn't. I went padding back up the tracks to the marshaling yard, where the rusty ghosts of old cars waited among the rank weeds.

I began to grow nervous now, approaching the old marshaling yard. Near the edge of the cliff beyond the last cars the ruined timbers of what must once have been one of the main shafts of the mine thrust up. I slowed, searching the grass ahead for bottomless pits, until I remembered that the man I had seen had run, not walked, following these same rusted steel rails. People didn't build railroad tracks over mine shafts. They weren't that crazy.

In my nervousness I had forgotten just where I had seen the man tugging at the lever of the switch I was looking for. All I remembered was that it was somewhere among these derelict cars ahead, and that he had disappeared among them almost immediately afterward. I found the memory frightening as I moved in among them. But when I turned my head, I could still see the road and the cut quite plainly.

Someone had just driven through the cut coming toward Glamis, for a mist of red dust still hung over the road and the cut, dust that hadn't been there when I found the greased points and the abandoned grease can over at the road. I couldn't see the car though. It must have reached Glamis, or the road near the entrance.

I shivered suddenly. Mr. McDonald had said anyone up here only had to look down to see us in the cut, and he was right about that. Anyone who looked down could have seen the car anywhere between Aberfeld and the entrance to Craig Glamis. And wasn't that the natural reaction, to look down before sending a runaway railroad car hurtling out of control down a long, steep grade?

Unless you were a potential murderer.

I jumped, and almost screamed in pure terror. Somewhere ahead, something had clanked distinctly, like the release or the joining of a coupling between cars.

I had stopped abruptly, my heart thudding while I listened, poised for flight. The sun had slid behind dark clouds borne up from the sea by a wind that seemed suddenly stronger.

It was darker between the derelict cars with the sun gone. There seemed suddenly more cars hemming me in, and deeper, darker shadows between them. I noticed for the first time that the tracks converged upon the area where I stood from the broken timbers and chutes of the old mine buildings. On either side of me the cars were still coupled end-to-end.

The sound came again, clearer, closer, coming from the line of cars on my right.

Someone, *something,* was moving the whole line of cars on my right toward me! The sounds were the clanking of the couplings. It seemed to me a task far beyond human strength. Yet here was no locomotive to move them, no sound of an engine's straining.

Clank, clank, clank. . . .

It happened again. And now the whole line of cars seemed moving toward me ever so slightly, but *moving* they were. I was sure of it now. I stared, frozen by fear. If a car had borne down upon me where I stood between the tracks, I could not have run away to save my life. And then, suddenly, I saw a different sort of movement. A figure appeared briefly between two of the cars a hundred yards away. It disappeared at once, its movements so furtive and so fast that all I had of it was the vague impression of human form. I began to sidle toward the cars on my left, not daring to look away from where that furtive, misshapen thing had disappeared. I found the end of the car by groping with my hand, and the nearest car did not seem to be coupled to it, so I could get through.

There was no other movement farther up the track, nothing that I could see or hear. And suddenly I found *that* even more frightening. *Because now I did not know where it was!*

The couplings no longer clanked, the cars no longer moved. There was no sound. Nothing. For all I knew, the figure I had seen could be creeping down the line of cars toward me. It had been a man, I decided, shuddering. And he might even have reached the car that I could touch by reaching out a hand. If he was behind it, I couldn't see him from where I stood. But he could see me by peering beneath the car. And if he knew I still stood here frozen, he could spring out from behind the car and . . .

The thought was too much for me, as I remembered that if this *was* the man I'd seen up here yesterday, he was a potential murderer.

It took effort to turn my back to him. With the flesh on the back of my neck creeping in anticipation of ruthless hands reaching for me, I bent and squirmed in between the two cars on my left. I was halfway through when I heard sound start behind me. Someone *had* been behind the cars; now whoever it was had emerged from hiding and was coming for me. I had been moving as soundlessly as I could, but fear whipped me now. I gasped and plunged forward, trying to escape, and felt my blouse catch in something that held me fast. Jammed where I was, I could not turn my body to see it, or reach it with my hand to free it in the confined space between two steel-walled cars. The blouse seemed to have been caught on the hook to which the coupling of the cars fastened when they were joined together.

While I tugged and squirmed frantically, I felt hands

take hold of me from behind, great strong hands that
tore at the trapped material so that my blouse was
jerked from the belt of my slacks and the seams tore
apart with a ripping sound. And he was laughing suddenly, a hoarse, terrifying male sound to which my
tortured senses attributed all the things I feared of him.
Triumph, cruelty, lust, murderous intent—that horrible
laughter held all these things, it seemed to me.

I screamed, and horror gave me strength, so that I
tore myself away from him, and felt the cloth rip again
as I fell forward away from the hook that had held me,
the cars that had trapped me, and those awful hands
that my abject terror pictured reaching to drag me back
to him. I sprang up and was running, hearing the weird
laughter stop while a hoarse voice called something after me that in my present state I could not understand.

Sobbing for breath, I shrieked as I ran. But he hadn't
given up. I could hear him running in pursuit of me on
the other side of the line of cars I followed. He ran
heavily, like a big man, like the kind of man I would
expect to have hands as strong as those that had torn
the cloth I could feel flapping behind me, as though it
were paper. And he could run *fast*. Already I could
hear him overtaking me. He was almost level with me
now, and if he drew ahead, if he reached the end of the
line of cars before me . . .

I no longer had breath for screaming. I had never
run so far or so fast in my life before. My blood
pounded in my ears. My lungs seemed bursting. Ahead,
the line of cars turned left as though converging again.
It occurred to me with horror that if our paths between
them converged as the cars were, they too must join.

I gave a last desperate cry. *"Help . . . me!"*

I was around the curve suddenly, seeing cars still in
line ahead, and hearing something I couldn't believe—
an answering shout.

"Tracey? Where are you, Tracey?"

There was someone standing between the cars ahead, a tall young man with dark hair who began to run toward me as I appeared. My eyes were blurring, my tortured breath failing now, but that was Peter McDonald running toward me.

"Peter . . . *help me!*" I gasped.

"Tracey, *look out!*" he shouted in alarm.

I saw the lever thrusting up from the weeds ahead that he was warning me about. I saw it without realizing that it was the switch I was seeking or that it too had been heavily greased. Nor did I realize that I had strayed too far among the derelict cars in my search for it. I saw the lever only as an obstacle that I must avoid because it stood in the path of my flight to Peter McDonald's reassuring presence.

I swerved around it through the grass, and the toe of my right shoe hooked beneath one of its iron rods, tripping me. I fell forward heavily, driving the last straining breath from my lungs so that I gasped vainly for air. I had the feeling of being held protectively in someone's arms while a voice I knew talked to me soothingly.

"It's all right, Tracey! You mustn't be afraid. There's nothing here that can harm you, darling."

I liked the things he was saying to me, and the anxiety for me that I heard quite plainly in his voice. But I wanted to tell Peter how wrong he was, for here at Glamis it seemed to me we were surrounded by the harm that evil people intended. I wanted to warn Peter that he too was in danger at this moment. Danger from a madman who moved railroad cars as though he had the strength of a Hercules. *A man who had tried to kill his father and me only yesterday!*

But though I tried, the words would not come out, and presently I was being lifted in his arms, until my lolling head rested against his shoulder while he strode with me toward the gates of Glamis. And somewhere on the way it all proved too much for me, so that complete darkness descended upon my mind and senses, and for a long time there was nothing. . . .

I struggled back slowly to reality, aware vaguely of familiar surroundings, and of some friendly presence close by. There had been voices somewhere that I remembered, discussing me and something they said I had imagined, and might imagine again. I remembered that I had felt resentment at the time because I _knew_ whatever it was they were discussing had really happened. Only now I couldn't remember what it was they'd been talking about.

I was in my room in the apartment in St. John, I decided. I must've been ill. The way I felt, I was still ill. So that must be my father sitting beside me, as he always had done to comfort me through the illnesses of childhood and adolescence. I opened my eyes and turned toward where he sat. He would be reading some book, his concentration absolute. And I would say . . . But I didn't speak or see him. I stared instead at a red-haired girl who looked so much like me that I thought I was dreaming, until recognition came, and with recognition, memory.

"Sandra?" I said.

She started, and turned to me quickly. "Tracey, are you all right?" She put down the magazine she held, and smiled at me. "It's good to see you awake! Is there anything I can get you?"

"No, thanks." I searched the room for someone else and was disappointed.

"He's gone," she said smiling. "He stayed with you as long as he could, but they called him from his office. One of his other patients is having a baby, and it couldn't wait. You *were* looking for Dr. McDonald, weren't you, Tracey?"

"I was just looking around," I lied irritably. "I didn't know *where* I was for a moment."

"You're beginning to sound more like yourself again," she said nastily. "He said I was to ask you how you felt when you woke up, and to leave a message at his office about that."

"You can tell him I feel fine, but I seem to have a sore arm." I added as it occurred to me, "And you can tell him I'm not imagining *that*." I sought the cause of the pain, and found some slight swelling and a small square of white tape stuck to the skin in the bend of my left elbow.

I was staring at it, puzzled, as she explained, "Peter gave you an injection. He said you'd been imagining things and needed a tranquilizer, and a strong one. He said it would make you sleep—and did it ever! You've been fast asleep ever since I came in here when Mrs. Brunier had to go downstairs to see about dinner."

"She stayed in here with me? Mrs. Brunier?"

She nodded. "She must like you. She was in here for hours. What happened to you, Tracey? She said you had a fall and were badly bruised. Peter said he found you wandering dazed in the old railroad yards near the mine. Someone should have told you it was dangerous to go there. What on earth were you doing there, anyhow?"

Wandering dazed? I stared at her angrily. "There was someone hiding among the old railroad cars. He *chased* me!"

She smiled. "Peter said you imagine things."

So it was *Peter* said that? "I suppose I imagined I tripped and fell too?" I said bitterly.

"Oh, no, he told Mrs. Brunier you did *that* when he called to you and you hurried toward him. He said you were lucky you didn't break your leg. He put something on your bruises when he put you to bed."

I became aware suddenly that I was wearing one of my nighties, a brief one at that, and that I had nothing on underneath it.

"*He* put me to bed?"

She laughed. "Don't you know that we women don't have any mystery for doctors, Tracey? They've seen it all! Yvonne Brunier undressed you, no doubt. She came upstairs with him when he carried you in like the young Lochinvar. Peter McDonald is the most eligible bachelor in these parts. He's very handsome, isn't he?"

"I haven't noticed," I lied. "Is he?"

" 'Is he?' Why can't things like that happen to poor little me?" she said disgustedly, getting up.

"They might if you threw away that silly red wig," I said. "It doesn't suit your coloring." I added as the thought occurred to me, "Did they persuade you to wear it because my mother had red hair? *That* wouldn't influence Uncle John."

"No, it was my idea," she said. "They'd always told me your mother had red hair, so one day in Halifax I tried this wig on to see what I'd look like with red hair. I found I like myself this way. Any objections?"

I shook my head. I was beginning to feel dizzy again. Maybe it was the injection still working.

She had walked over to my mirror and started admiring herself while she patted her phony red hair into place. She said over her shoulder, "Since you're awake and yourself again now, you can do without me. I'll call Peter from my room and tell him you're awake and feel fine except for his clumsiness with a needle."

I wondered if that was all she wanted to tell Peter. I said quickly, "There's a phone in here."

She straightened, and smiled at her reflection. "Sorry to disappoint you, cousin, but I'm going. You know, we *are* alike, when I'm wearing this thing. Maybe we should buy identical clothes and go out together. People would take us for twins."

"Yuk!" I muttered, and she giggled and left me.

I closed my eyes and waited for the room to steady again. It was later than I had thought, I decided. I could hear my coal fire crackling cheerfully behind its screen where Beth had organized it for the night. I opened my eyes and found the small traveling clock my father had given me one Christmas in its place on the bedside table. I couldn't quite believe what its hands showed as I wound it and put it back in place. It was already eleven o'clock. Downstairs the lights would be going out soon, except for the chandelier in the passage that burned all night.

As I thought about that, the light in the passage outside my door went out abruptly, and I saw that Sandra, as I might have expected, had left my bedroom door wide open. After what had happened today, I wanted that door *locked*. And the windows too, even if fumes from the burning coal choked me, as Beth had warned they might unless I left a window open. I sat up and realized for the first time how wrung out I really felt after all that had happened to me. It took all my strength just to get out of bed, and I was unsteady on my feet as I forced myself to the door and closed and locked it. For good measure, I thrust home the big old-fashioned bolt that should have stopped a battering ram.

I had to stay there leaning against the door for quite a while before I could find strength to check my windows. They were both partly open as I stared out nervously. There seemed nothing close enough on either side or above to enable a prowler to reach them. I leaned over the sill and stared down, finding the ground much farther below me than I'd expected, and nothing but the smooth stone wall between. I seemed safe from anyone outside, and there was nothing to fear from the passage, so I left one window open at the top as a safety precaution against the carbon monoxide.

Before I turned back to my bed, I stared out over the wall at the sea. A ship was passing far out; a liner I supposed, since it was ablaze with lights. The sea was dark except for those moving lights, with an edge of moon showing among ragged cloud, and few stars to be seen. I shivered in air that seemed colder than it had been today, and reached for the drapes to draw them closed, and froze with my hands gripping them.

Beneath the wall of Glamis, a light had come on abruptly in the dark museum.

Staring across, I felt myself shiver. Ralph Craig had talked about a light like this one that had come on so suddenly far back within the building. I stared across the lawns at it, trembling. It seemed far back from the windows that faced me. It was in some smaller room with an open door, I decided. A room that must be right at the back of the building close to the wall itself, it seemed so far away.

As I studied it, I saw furtive movement start. Far back, *something* was crossing between the light and me. It moved slowly into focus and vision. A figure that seemed misshapen and only vaguely human.

The light went out, and it was gone.

I was scurrying back to my bed suddenly, my weakness forgotten. I tore aside the covers and crawled beneath them, to lie there shaking with the covers drawn right up to my chin.

The figure I had seen against the light was the same I had seen in the marshaling yard!

Chapter *SIX*

———— ◆◆ ◆ ◆————

I wakened from troubled and uneasy sleep to the clatter of cups somewhere in the passage outside, as Beth brought the morning coffee. My fire had died to a few glowing coals, and it was stuffy in the big bedroom. I climbed stiffly from my bed and pulled on a robe. Beyond the window drapes the early-morning sun shone from a clear sky, and cod boats were busily fishing far out. The happenings of last night and yesterday seemed far off and easily forgotten this morning.

I had the door unbolted and my windows open before Beth arrived, smiling, with my coffee.

She chattered about the household as she fussed around. Uncle John had come back late last night, and Mrs. Brunier had to serve him a late supper because he seldom ate out these days. And then in the small hours of the morning Donald Craig had come home and couldn't find his key and wakened everyone downstairs hammering at the door of the housekeeper's apartment before Mrs. Brunier got out of bed to let him in. She hinted that Donald had been pretty high, which didn't surprise me. I liked Donald even less than I liked his brother, Ralph, and Donald didn't like me either, since I'd refused the cocktail he put together my first night at Craig Glamis.

I smiled and interrupted the flow of her gossip. "Does Mrs. Brunier have an apartment? It's not just a suite like this?"

"We call it her apartment. It's separate from the

79

house, and quite private. Mr. Craig had it built specially for her above the garages when her son was born. The garages were once stables, but her apartment is quite modern."

"She said she had a son. How old is he, Beth?"

She shrugged. "None of us would know. About our age, maybe. Twenty. Have you met him yet?"

"No, I haven't."

"She keeps him out of sight," she said, lowering her voice. "We seldom see Ivan. Your Uncle John lets him work in the museum with Ralph and Sandra. I think he figures that keeps Ivan out of mischief by giving him something to do. And Mrs. Brunier keeps him under wraps in the apartment the rest of the time, which is oka with us. He's *weird*! Downstairs, we girls sleep w the shutters bolted even in summer."

I stared at her. "You mean he's . . . dangerous to g ?"

to prove that with Ivan?" she said. "Wait till you see him. He's a creep! He's never harmed any of us physically, though. Not *yet*. But only a few months ago, Ruth, one of the kitchen maids, came home late from a date in Aberfeld and woke us all up screaming her head off. She'd forgotten to close her shutters, and she saw Ivan at the window watching her undress. He was gone when everyone came running, of course. And when your uncle went over to the apartment and woke his mother, he was fast asleep in bed. He was foxing for sure! It wasn't the first time something like that had happened. He's always spying on us one way or another."

"It couldn't have been someone else? Some prowler? Did Uncle report it to the police?"

"Your uncle didn't. He has a hang-up about Ivan, and of course Mrs. Brunier is Ivan's mother. So they're both always sure it wasn't Ivan—even before they start checking. And he's so quick, he could run through walls! It's incredible how he gets out of things, so all we ever hear is that he's asleep, or working in the museum. It's a waste of time complaining, I'll tell you."

"You said Uncle John has a hang-up about him?" I asked, frowning.

She nodded. "You don't know about Ivan, then? He was born here at Glamis in midwinter. They were snowed in, and there was a blizzard when she went into labor. The doctor from Aberfeld couldn't get here, so your uncle delivered the baby with the help of your mother. It was a difficult birth, they say. And your mother and your uncle were only amateurs. So something went wrong, and the baby's head and spine were injured."

"She said he was retarded!" I remembered.

Beth nodded. "In some ways he's still like a little boy, though your uncle sent him to all sorts of specialists. Anyhow, that's the way it is with Ivan, Miss Craʲ Is there anything else I can do for you before I goʳᵛ were all very sorry to hear about your fall, whᵢ Mrs. Brunier told us about it downstairs yesteʳday. You should have your bath while it's hot. It will help the stiffness."

"Thanks," I said, my mind still on what she had told me. "We should feel sorry for someone like that. Ivan can't help what happened."

"I do," she said. "When Ivan isn't scaring me half to death, I could almost like him. But not quite, Miss Craig. I keep remembering that he isn't really a boy, he's a man. And as strong as any two men I know. So one of these days, maybe just looking at us won't be enough to satisfy Ivan. And if he did attack one of the girls . . . well, what could she *do* about it?"

I shook my head. I was remembering big, strong

hands upon me in the marshaling yard yesterday. Hands that had torn the strong cloth of my blouse like paper.

"None of us would go near the old railroad tracks for anything, Miss Craig," Beth said, collecting my empty cup. "I hope you keep away from there from now on. You were lucky Dr. McDonald noticed you there as he drove up the hill."

So that was how Peter had happened to hear me screaming! "Don't worry, Beth, I *won't* go near that place again!" I said with feeling. I was still thinking of the fright I'd had, thinking of hands that I was identifying now with Mrs. Brunier's retarded son. I added, "You mean because of Ivan, don't you? Does he go there often?"

She stared at me. "They don't allow Ivan outside Glamis gates, unless your uncle or his mother goes with him. Sometimes they take him to Sydney to buy clothes, or to a doctor in Halifax, who examines him once a year. And I'll say this for him—he never attempts to leave the grounds."

I stared at her. "No?"

"Never." She smiled. "We can walk down to Aberfeld at night, or along the cliffs in summer, and never need think of him. I meant the mine shafts. If you'd fallen into one of those, we'd never see you again."

"I never went *near* the mine buildings!" I said.

She shook her head. "It's ventilation shafts *I* mean, Miss Craig. The shafts that helped circulate air through the old workings. There are half a dozen such shafts hidden under the long grass in the old railroad yard. They were timbered over when the mine closed, but that was year ago. Who knows what's happened to them now? They could be open and waiting to swallow one of us. And them so hidden and grown over you'd never know they were there till you stepped on rotten wood, or nothing, and down you went like a bundle of clothes in the linen chute, never to be seen or heard of again."

I stared after her in dismay as she went out with her tray. I was remembering blundering about in the long grass there yesterday. It could have happened to *me*, the way she said

The door closed, and she was gone. I got into my bath, but even soaking the pain from bruises and strained muscles couldn't get yesterday out of my mind. I had to *tell* someone about it. I wanted to tell Peter McDonald, but I remembered that yesterday he wouldn't believe there had been any danger for me there. Lying back in my bath, I scowled at the ceiling and told Peter I hated him, even if he had called me darling at the time and carried me in his arms from that awful place where someone that everyone else refused to believe existed had tried to kill his father and me, and then frightened me almost to death.

I could find other faults with Peter too if I tried, I decided. Like how unreliable he was, not coming to see me yesterday morning, even if being late *had* meant he was there to save me when I needed him most. In fact, it was astonishing how a man who looked so fantastic could *have* so many faults. It was a pity he wasn't more like his father, even though Angus had scared me with his sinister looks when he appeared unannounced at my father's funeral. But at least Angus had seen danger for me here from greedy relations.

If I must talk to someone, why not Angus, whom my father trusted, even though Angus had disliked him for twenty years? I was going to talk to Angus McDonald, I decided abruptly. And I was going to talk to him *right now!*

I scrambled out of my bath, and still dripping, wrapped myself in a bath towel like a sari and went to the phone. Dialing, I pretended I wasn't hoping

Peter would answer. He didn't. It was a woman's voice, a rich contralto made even more attractive by the Scottish brogue.

When I identified myself, she said, "They told me I was to fetch one of them immediately you called, Miss Craig. Hold the line and I'll have one of the men here in a moment."

I murmured thanks. It would be Peter who would answer, I decided, and he would be sympathetic and friendly this morning. I, on the other hand, would be coldly distant as I told him that I wanted to speak to his father about what happened to me yesterday, since there seemed no point in discussing anything like that with him.

"Is that you, Tracey?"

It was a different woman's voice, younger, vaguely familiar. "Who is that?" I demanded.

She giggled. "Sandra, of course. Why?"

"What are you doing at the McDonalds'? I thought *you* were still in bed," I protested, jolted from my thoughts by recognition of her. "And do you mind? I'm speaking to someone!"

"I know," she said. "To Mrs. McDonald, and you're waiting for Angus—or *is* it Peter? I thought you'd like to know I gave Peter your message last night. Remember? You told me to tell him you felt fine—except for the way he hurt you giving you the tranquilizer injection."

"I don't know what I said to you last night," I told her indignantly. "I'd just opened my eyes, and I wasn't feeling well. Now, would you mind getting Mrs. McDonald back for me? And then, *get off the line!* I want to speak to the McDonalds privately."

"Anything you say, Tracey," she said, and the phone clicked as she put it down.

"Sandra!"

Of all the fool girls! Now I'd have to call the McDonalds again. And she'd cut me off from spite, I was sure of it. I was moving to put my own phone down when a voice I knew said abruptly from the phone, "You wanted me, Tracey?"

"Mr. McDonald! I thought we'd been cut off."

"Mrs. McDonald had to fetch me, Tracey. I was in my study. Where are you calling from? Glamis?"

"Yes, from my bedroom. I just got up. I wanted to tell you—"

His harsh voice interrupted me rudely. "If it concerns the matter I spoke to you about when I gave you my card, you don't have to tell me anything. Everything is under control now. In a few days at most I expect to be able to answer whatever questions you have about the matter."

I stared at the phone. "I'm afraid I don't quite understand."

"Peter brought me up-to-date about you last night. He thought you might call. He said you seemed very nervous after your fall."

"Look, it wasn't just the fall," I said indignantly "That is what I want to discuss with you. Someone tried—"

"Of course it wasn't just the fall, Tracey!" he interrupted me rudely again. "Your nervousness, Peter and I agreed, is the result of a number of things. Too much has happened to you in the space of a few days."

"You can say that again!" If the only way I could have my say with him was by interruption, I'd show him I could be as rude as he was. "And yesterday among the railroad cars near the old mine, someone—"

"Your father's death came into it," he said, as though he hadn't heard. "You were brought suddenly into a completely new environment, where we had a nasty accident. And now you have another fall that knocks you unconscious. It's no wonder you're nervous and expecting unpleasant things to happen. But there's no need. You have friends. You're not alone. And I've just assured you that the matter we discussed when you came to Glamis is being taken care of now. Tracey, I have a case being dealt with in the Equity Court at Halifax this afternoon I must go now."

"But, Mr. McDonald," I protested in dismay, "I haven't even told you—"

"Peter had to go out on a case in the middle of his breakfast this morning," he said. "He told his mother he intended to visit you immediately afterward, so he should be knocking on your door any moment now. If you have any problems concerning your nervousness, why don't you discuss them with him? I merely look after people's legal problems. Good day to you, Tracey."

"But you wouldn't even listen to me! I wanted to tell you that . . ." I broke off in dismay. *"Mr. Mc-Donald!"* He was already gone.

I jammed my phone furiously back on its cradle. Of all the dogmatic old . . . Angus McDonald was worse than his son, Peter. Much worse! I'd been right the first time about *him,* I decided, my mind seeing him again as a sinister figure standing in a cemetery in the rain. I began to suspect he had some part in the terrifying things happening to me, even if he had been involved with me in the first dreadful incident of the runaway coal car. A cold, calculating man like him might be involved in anything for profit.

In imagination I began to picture Angus McDonald as another infamous Macbeth intent on my murder for his profit, though where the profit could be in it for Angus, I couldn't decide. And then suddenly I remembered what he had said about Peter coming here to see me. Here I was wearing only a damp bath towel! Even as I sprang up from my chair at the telephone, I heard footsteps coming from the stairs toward my room. Out there Mrs. Brunier was talking to someone who replied in a deep, pleasant voice.

Peter!

I gasped, and with my anger and suspicions forgotten, rushed for the clothes closet as someone knocked on my door.

"You'll have to wait! I won't be long!" I called in consternation.

"It doesn't matter if you're still in bed, Miss Craig," the housekeeper's voice assured me. "It's Dr. McDonald here to see you. You don't need to get up. I have a key."

"Dr. McDonald will have to wait, I've just come from the shower," I called back in alarm. "*Wait!* I'll let you in. . . ." I compromised by grabbing a nightie and my robe and slippers again. I had pulled the robe too tightly around me as I let them in, and his first glance was far from being a professional one. I loosened it again hurriedly before I closed the door behind them.

"How do you feel this morning, Miss Craig?"

I tried not to like his friendly smile as I told him. The way I felt about the McDonalds, I'd as soon have smiled at Judas. But he looked pleased when I said I felt fine.

"No problems with the arm this morning?"

Taken by surprise, I said, "No. Why?"

"The way I heard it, you had bone damage at the least where the needle I gave you went in." He smiled.

So Sandra had told him. I muttered something about people exaggerating these things, and felt guilty as he made Mrs. Brunier help me onto my bed and cover me with a sheet while he made his examination. I noticed the first thing he looked at was the needle mark, which looked no worse than a tiny red spot on the vein beneath the white surgical patch.

"Looks healthy enough," he said, squeezing a touch of penicillin cream on a new white square and replacing the old one. "But then, so do you. Any discomfort from the bruising? No? Good. Any headache this morning?"

"No, doctor."

He nodded. "No damage that you can notice, eh? Well, I might as well check one or two other things while I'm here."

"The bruises feel fine, doctor," I said hurriedly, grasping my robe defensively as I remembered that some of my bruises were in embarrassing places.

He smiled. "That wasn't what I had in mind, Miss Craig," he told me, getting his stethoscope ready to auscultate my chest. You would've thought he was examining me for insurance. I mean, what does taking your blood pressure, pulse, and temperature, listening to your breathing and heartbeat, and staring into your eyes through an ophthalmoscope have to do with falling on your head and knocking yourself out?

But eventually he finished, and nodded as though satisfied. "You'll be relieved to know I can find no damage at all, Miss Craig," he said. "Which is more than you deserve, or I expected. That was quite a fall you took, you know."

"What about the lump on my head, doctor?" I asked, feeling cut down to size.

"It's nothing to worry you," he said calmly. "The skin isn't broken. If it's uncomfortable, a cold pad with some pressure will disperse it more quickly. But I don't believe you'll need that. I think it will be gone by tomorrow morning, without any aftereffects."

That wasn't the way it felt to me after his prodding, but I buttoned my nightie where he'd loosened it at the throat, and sat up. He looked at Mrs. Brunier and smiled. "I'm keeping you, Yvonne, when I know you're needed downstairs for breakfast. I'm going to write her a prescription for some tablets before I leave, so you can go on down if you wish. I'll see Mr. Craig while I'm up here, and come down with him later."

She gave him a suspicious glance from dark eyes, as though she was sure he intended my seduction. "I will send Beth Cartwright up to take my place, doctor."

"Mr. Craig prefers being alone with me. He doesn't like any of you around while I'm checking him, Yvonne. I thought you knew that."

"I do," she said grimly. "But I wasn't thinking of him. I was thinking of Miss Craig." Her quick glance was to reassure me, I supposed, as she added, "I'll send Beth, doctor."

He shrugged and said, "Please yourself. It makes no difference to me."

I watched Yvonne Brunier go out, leaving the door open deliberately behind her. I had no doubt that that was intended as further protection for me, and supposed I should be grateful, but wasn't sure that I was.

Peter McDonald got up and went over to close the door quietly and come back to me. "I have to talk to you privately, Tracey," he said. "And you must listen to me for once without trying to tell me what you think is happening here."

"You don't even know what happened to me yesterday," I blurted angrily. "You won't listen, or if you do, you don't believe me! Neither does your father. I phoned him not half an hour ago, and—"

"Will you listen?" he demanded fiercely. "I'm trying to help you, Tracey . . . and we don't have much time."

He had put his hands on my shoulders as though he meant to shake me into silence. He released me again as suddenly. "Sometimes you make me mad!" he said.

I nodded a little shakily, aware that he had hurt my shoulders. "That goes double!" I said. "But if it's so important—go on. What is it?"

"*Please just listen*, can't you?" he gritted. "When Dad gave you his card when you were upset about what happened on the road, and I told you if Dad didn't come and get you out of here when you needed help, *I* would—there was something we both forgot."

"There was?"

"That's right." He scowled at me suddenly. "Did you say you *phoned* Dad? What did you say to him?"

"I tried to tell him about what happened to me yesterday, of course." Just remembering made me angry. "He wouldn't listen. He interrupted me each time I tried to tell him. He was most rude."

"You mean he wouldn't let you *say* what you intended?"

"I told you. He just kept interrupting. He was very rude. In the end, he might just as well have hung up on me, the abrupt way he ended our conversation."

"Good old Dad!" he said. "So maybe it's all right! Did he say anything about me?"

"Only that if I had any nervous problems I should tell you, not him. The way he said it, you'd think I was neurotic and had made the whole thing up."

"Okay," he said. "I'll talk to him later; he'll know whether you blurted anything out that could be disastrous to you. Now, you listen. In this house, when anyone calls out to Aberfeld or anywhere else, the sound of the outgoing call being made registers faintly on all the other phones in the house. It means that anyone who is curious about you for any reason whatsoever has merely to pick up another phone quietly and hear everything you say."

"Sandra talked to me while I was waiting for your father!" I remembered angrily. "I couldn't get rid of her. I thought she was at your house in Aberfeld! But she did put her phone down. I heard, and thought she'd cut us off. Then your dad spoke."

"She was here," he said disgustedly. "And you can bet she wasn't the only one listening in!"

I stared at him. "You can't blame me for not knowing that! The only time you can listen to someone else's phone conversation where I come from is when the lines are crossed And then you can't talk *to* them, and you don't know who or where they are, unless they obligingly tell the other party that."

"Here at Glamis you can carry on a family conference with every phone tuned in," he said. "I'm not blaming you for not knowing that, Tracey—I'm blaming Dad and myself for not telling you. But maybe there's no harm done. Dad is a very good attorney. He *may* have been able to stop you from saying too much. So, maybe . . . nothing."

He'd contrived to make it sound as though I talked too much. "If that was all you wanted to say," I said, "maybe you'll listen to *me* now. Yesterday I proved that someone greased the switch and the points so they could—"

"We know all that!" he said impatiently. "I wish you'd stop playing detective before you really get hurt! None of us want that to happen, Tracey, believe me "

"*Someone* does!" I retorted angrily. "Yesterday he—"

"Not now, Tracey!" he said, interrupting me as rudely as his father. "Listen. *If* you need to talk to us, and it isn't a matter of life and death, as your imagination seems making you think everything that happens around Glamis is, why not just come down to Aberfeld? It isn't far, and all you have to do to get there is ask Yvonne to send the car to the front entrance to pick you up. You're not a *prisoner*. But if you have a real emergency, use the phone in your uncle's study. It's a special line, so nobody can listen in—he saw to that. And the key to the study is always kept on the *inside*, so that he can lock it when working if he's so inclined. *Remember that!* It means you can lock yourself in."

"I'll remember, but—"

"No buts!" he said, lowering his voice. "One more thing. The reason we know more than you do about what is happening at Glamis is because Dad has had someone investigating the situation here for some time now. His name is Paul Garrick, and he's a private investigator who works for Dad in Montreal and Quebec. Paul has been instructed to look after you since the attempt was made with the railroad car"

"So where was he yesterday?" I said indignantly.

"He . . ." He broke off and tore a page from the pad he had been scribbling on. "Beth is coming. Take this and have them get the tablets in Aberfeld for you. Take one at bedtime. And remember, not a word to anyone about Paul Garrick, or you could get him killed."

"What about me?" I hissed at him angrily. "Someone tried to kill *me* again yesterday. In the railroad yard near the old mine. I tried to tell you, but you wouldn't listen. Why did you think I was running? Did you think I was so pleased to see you that I ran into your arms? How do you think my clothes got torn? He grabbed me in there, but I got away from him, and—"

"This really happened?" He was staring at me suddenly with belief in his eyes, his face growing angry.

"He tore the blouse I was wearing! Do you want to see it?"

"I saw it last night," he muttered, scowling. "But I thought you tore it when you fell. So this guy actually attacked you? That means you saw him. We need to know about this——"

"If you can take time to listen!" Out in the passage now I could hear Beth at the door.

He picked up his doctor's bag, and I watched him walk to the door. "Don't forget your tablet," he said, opening the door for the maid. He smiled at her. "I was just going, Beth. Do you know if Mr. Craig is still in his bedroom?"

Beth gave him a seductive smile. "He's waiting for you, doctor."

She watched him admiringly for a long moment as he walked away, before she came inside. I glared angrily at the prescription he had put into my hand. I thought maybe I could use sedation tonight. . . .

She was staring into space like a girl I'd known at college who used to do that every time she heard the Rolling Stones. I brought Beth back cruelly to the present.

"Did Mrs. Brunier send you to stay with me while Dr. McDonald was here, Beth?"

"Yes, Miss Craig," she murmured dreamily.

"In that case, I don't need you, do I? Dr. McDonald left as you came in."

She looked at me, startled, seeing *me* suddenly now, instead of whatever had filled her mind. "I'm sorry, Miss Craig! I was daydreaming."

"Dr. McDonald seems to have that effect on you," I said acidly. "Doesn't he?"

She sighed. "Not only on me, Miss Craig. Half the girls in Aberfeld drool about Dr. McDonald. Not that he ever looks at them either."

"I don't know what you see in him," I lied.

She shook her head. Obviously she couldn't understand why he failed to attract me. "He's handsome, tall, nice to people. Miss Craig, he's just about got *every-*

thing, the way we look at it. But of course, if you don't happen to fancy tall, dark, and handsome men . . . I mean, every girl's taste *is* a little different where romance is concerned, isn't it?"

I nodded. She had a point there. "If you don't mind, I'll dress now."

"I'm going, Miss Craig." She got halfway to the door and stopped abruptly and came back. "Miss Craig, I'm sorry! I had a message for you from your Uncle John. He said he has to go to the mines again today, but he would like you to go to the museum this morning with Miss Sandra. But he doesn't want you to work there until he has discussed it with you."

I frowned. Yesterday I would have been delighted, but today I couldn't find much that was attractive in the idea of being with Sandra. She was just too sneaky. She'd proved that this morning by listening in to the conversation I'd been trying to have with Angus McDonald. And Ralph seemed little better. I had no doubt Ralph would have been listening in too if he knew what I was doing. Still, it was better than doing nothing.

"Does he expect me to see him about it before he leaves? Or call him?"

"Goodness no," she said, smiling again now. "He'd hate that, Miss Craig. When he has a business deal on, he doesn't want to be bothered with details about anything else. He'll just expect you to do as he said."

I nodded. "Very well. I'll do that, Beth. Thank you."

She giggled suddenly. "Fancy me almost forgetting your message like that! It just shows you how Dr. McDonald affects us, doesn't it?"

"I'm glad I'm not one of you!" I told her bitterly.

Before dressing, I drew the shades, and stared down at the museum before I closed the last gap. I shivered suddenly, remembering the grotesque figure I'd seen in there at night, the same figure I was sure I had glimpsed

between the railroad cars. Remembering, I could feel
again the strength of hands with fingers of iron tearing
at my thick clothing while I struggled like a trapped
and frightened young animal.

I shuddered and drew the drapes against the watching eyes I imagined. I went hurriedly for my clothes,
choosing plain things. Remembering I'd worn slacks
yesterday, I chose a white woolen midi-length frock today. It was warm and not too figure-molding, and had
sleeves that were full at the elbows and narrowed at
the wrists. The neck was high, almost a crew neck.

By the time I went down to breakfast, I had re-
gained confidence and calm again.

Chapter *SEVEN*

———— ••◦••◦•• ————

"In the fifteenth century, nobles, scholars, and wealthy men took part in the revival of the collection of rare and beautiful objects from ancient times, Tracey," Ralph Craig told me sententiously. "In the next two centuries, many private art collections, coin and medal collections, weapon collections, and all kinds of other collections of rare and valuable curiosities were established by individuals throughout Europe. Historically, the modern museums, private or otherwise, sprang from these beginnings. Uncle John is famous as a collector of medieval things. If you see more weapons and armor than anything, it's because people of that day were forced to use them continually to survive."

"I'm glad I live now," I said.

He glanced at me. "What's so different? When one reads about the things happening today, it makes you wonder if the world will ever become civilized. Personally, I doubt it. See this cast-iron pot? It can be tipped by lifting the handle. Receptacles like this were spaced along the battlements of castles. Pitch was kept boiling in them by small fires lit beneath them, and when attackers raised their ladders and began to climb the castle walls, the defenders tilted the handle and the boiling pitch poured over them."

"Yuk!" I said.

"Today we get the same effect on a much larger scale with napalm," he said grimly. "Which must seem much the same to the victim. Brutality and violence are going on all over the world today, only on a greater scale, because of the population explosion."

I studied his face as we walked along the rows of armor and weapons on display. "I didn't know you felt that way."

"Then you know now, Tracey," he said curtly. "I hate the thought of violence in any form. I always have. And I always will. I'll have to go to work now in the restoration room we call the workshop. Ivan's in there, and you'll need to meet him. Sandra will show you the rest of the museum when she gets here. I'll call her from the workshop and hurry her along. In the meantime, I suggest you just browse with the catalog I gave you. And after Sandra has shown you the chamber and the other rooms, you can spend as long as you like on your orientation. We'll be here all day, except for the break for lunch."

"Office hours?"

He smiled. "More or less. When a new shipment comes in, Uncle John works us hard. We have one in now, but since he isn't here, we're conserving our strength for when he is. You'll find out when he gets back from his conference."

I was seeing a different side to Ralph this morning, some of it surprising. I felt better about him for what he had said about hating violence in any form. If that was true—and he seemed sincere to me—I had nothing to fear from him.

"What is in there?"

It was a closed door, a double door like the one at the entrance to the museum. The double door seemed to me to indicate space and importance within.

He glanced at it with distaste. "That's the chamber. I seldom go in there. Ivan looks after its artifacts. It's Uncle John's specialty, and the *pièce de résistance* of the museum so far as his fellow collectors are concerned. You can go in if you want to, but it would be better to go with Sandra and have the purpose of some of the implements explained to you. Ivan could do that better than any of us, but he'd have trouble communicating with a girl like you. I'm afraid he's never had anything to do with girls, and he has a very real hang-up about that, it seem to me. He never goes to Aberfeld, and the girls here disappear when they see Ivan coming."

"Do they have reason?" I was thinking about what Beth had said suddenly.

"Not in my opinion," Ralph said shortly. "Ivan mightn't be like you and me, but he'd never *hurt* anyone. And certainly not girls. Girls are an unknown quantity to him, and so he's afraid of you. And even Sandra, who should know better, helps that fear along by her attitude toward him."

I frowned at a Moorish soldier staring at me murderously from beneath his helmet, curved sword in hand. This part of the museum reminded me of Madame Tussaud's waxworks as described in one of Dad's books. Except Uncle John's models looked far more sinister to me.

"Sandra said he spies on people," I suggested.

He frowned at me. "So he's curious about girls," he said. "So what? Who isn't at some time or other in their early life? With him, though, it's the result of growing to manhood in a separate compartment where he has no real contact with anyone, except your Uncle John, his mother, and me. He has skill with his hands. Some of the intricate restoration he does, I'm damned sure nobody else here *could* do. But Ivan doesn't *think* as we do."

"Is he really badly retarded?"

"He has the mind of a gentle and rather simple boy

of ten or twelve," Ralph said. "You might remember that when you meet him."

"I'll try," I promised doubtfully.

"Maybe later, if you can win his confidence, Ivan will tell you about the chamber. It fascinates him, as it probably would most boys of his mental age with a taste for adventure."

He hadn't stopped, so I'd walked on with him past the door of what he had called the "chamber." "What sort of chamber is it" I asked, looking back. "I mean, what does my uncle keep in there?"

"Implements of torture," he said grimly. "The chamber is an exact replica of a medieval torture chamber your uncle discovered in a castle in Spain. He bought the contents, shipped them here for restoration, and had the inner chamber reconstructed from plans made of the Spanish one."

I shuddered involuntarily. "For heaven's sake, *why*?"

"Because except possibly for one or two of the great museums of Europe, you won't find its like anywhere else," he said. "Tomás de Torquemada, the infamous Dominican prior who became Grand Inquisitor and head of the Holy Office of the Inquisition, used it to torture heretics into confessing imaginery sins that earned them the death by burning of the *auto-da-fe*. That was from 1483 on, during the most hideous years of the Inquisition. And the Spanish nobleman, so called, whose descendants' castle the original chamber was found in, used it to torture and kill his personal enemies or wring money from the few surviving wealthy Jews in *his* territory when Torquemada and his executioners weren't using it. An example that the Spaniard's descendants followed ruthlessly for generations."

"I'm not sure I *want* to see it, Ralph!" I said.

He nodded. "I understand how you feel about the chamber, Tracey," he said. "I feel the same way about it. The implements in there are real, not toys. They killed and tortured people with a cruelty we can't even match today. But if you work here on cataloging, every now and then you're going to have to go in there for Uncle John. So you might as well get used to it."

He had stopped at a door at the far end of the museum, marked "Staff Only." He held it open for me politely, and followed me inside. He looked around quickly.

"Ivan?"

"He must've gone out for a moment," I said. "Isn't that where he's been working? At the other table?"

"It's where he *should* be working," Ralph Craig growled. "This is part of the shipment we're unpacking."

"Are they beads?"

He nodded, and picked up the card lying beside them and checked. "Onyx beads, probably of Roman origin, but worn in thirteenth-century Britain by a young woman of quality. Her skeleton, together with the skeletons of two men, was found beside one of the old Roman roads. A Roman sesterce, a coin worth a quarter of a denarius, was found with them. Tests on the bones establish the approximate age of the artifacts and the year of death of the victims. The three persons were apparently traveling toward Bath when they were attacked, murdered, and robbed. The fact that nothing else was found there indicates robbery. The single coin and the beads were an oversight, or perhaps the killers were disturbed. The bodies were hastily buried in the ditch beside the road, either by the attackers or by other travelers who found them and were afraid of being blamed for their deaths."

"The card says all that?"

He grinned and showed it to me. "Onyx beads," I read. "Roman sesterce. (See separate card.) Found

1878 near three skeletons, one female twenty years, two males thirty to forty years. Found on site of Roman road, Bath, England. Men's skulls damaged. Woman intact. Bone tests indicate thirteenth century. From collection of Signor Spelleti, Florence, Italy, to Craig Museum, Glamis, Aberfeld, N.S., Canada."

I frowned at him. "You made it sound like a detective story."

He grinned. "We have to use deduction. But when you think about it, what I told you is probably what happened. And Uncle John likes to get an approximate story of the origin of the artifact, which we show only as such on the cards we use here. Mainly we try to work out why they were found where they were found—unless the artifact already has an established history. The artifacts in the chamber, for instance, are fully authenticated. We can trace them from their construction, and even know the names of some of the victims and those torturers whom Torquemada thought most skillful."

"Will he expect me to do things like that? I mean, like you did just now?" I asked, interested.

"Probably," he said. "But let me warn you . . . you'd better consider the evidence carefully before you commit your deductions to paper. He'll tear a strip off you if he thinks you're wrong. So don't make any snap approximations of what happened, like I did to amuse you just now."

"I thought you were very good," I said, surprised. "The Roman women did use onyx beads as jewelry. It was one of their most popular gemstones. So it figures the beads came from Rome, and were made there. The male skulls were damaged; that indicates fighting. A woman, in this case either a noble Norman woman or noble Briton, wouldn't travel without guards. Burial in the ditch beside the road indicates haste on the part of the men who killed her and her companions. The haste indicates fear of the consequences of their act, and seems more likely the work of outlaws than anyone else. To clinch what you deduced, it couldn't have been a Roman woman, because of the test that indicated the age of the bones as thirteenth-century." I smiled, pleased with my reasoning.

He shook his head at me. "I was quite wrong," he said. "And Uncle John would be the first to tell me so. There was probably no connection whatever between the three skeletons and the coin and necklace. The coin and the necklace could have been lying there since the Roman occupation of Britain, and how they got there we'll never know. The three skeletons left nothing behind because they had nothing. They were just poor Britons, ragged serfs, the men murdered by passing Norman soldiery for the woman, whose skeleton, remember, was undamaged. When they'd finished with her, they cut her throat and threw her in the ditch with the dead men."

I stared at him, shocked, but recognizing the fault in his earlier reasoning and in mine.

"I hate violence!" he said angrily. "Even talking about it. But things like that were happening all over Europe and Britain in the thirteenth century. Where the hell is Ivan? Playing hookey in the woods behind the house or back in the apartment raiding his mother's kitchen? Or maybe he's in the chamber? These are his favorite things anytime he escapes from here! I'll have to start work, Tracey. Would you mind looking in the chamber for him? If he's in there, tell him I want him. Don't stare at him, or you'll embarrass him, and we'll be lucky to get him back here all today."

I frowned. "I wouldn't embarrass anyone handicapped like that, not intentionally," I told him. "But it *would* help if I knew what to expect when I see him."

He had gone over to the first table and sat down. He looked up at me, his mind already on a jeweled dagger he was taking from its wrappings, which with its card awaited his attention. "I thought you knew," he muttered. "Ivan is a hunchback, Tracey. He's been that way since birth."

Since his birth one icy night here at Glamis, I remembered with a shock. With no doctor or midwife to attend the mother, only Uncle John and my mother to help a terrified woman bring Ivan Brunier into the world.

I closed the workshop door behind me and looked around. I'd been nervous and uncertain on finding only Ralph here when I came in earlier. But I had to admit that he'd been quite nice to me this morning, and in his own way had seemed trying to help me fit in here. Yet being alone with him in the museum had kept me on edge, so that despite his running commentary on what he had been showing me, I hardly knew now what I'd seen.

I stared around curiously. It looked like a museum anywhere, I guess. Except that here the exhibits were principally from the Middle Ages. In the glass-topped display cases were examples of the art and culture of Europe from the reign of the Roman Emperor Justinian to the Renaissance. Around the walls, as though guarding far more precious exhibits in the showcases, were the weapons and armor of men-at-arms, crusading knights, Saracens, Visigoths, and Britons. Here and there, to display them, stood models so lifelike that they made me nervous.

I supposed I'd get used to those fierce, cruel soldiers of another age, with their gruesome tools of war. In the showcases were the things that mattered to me more. I could spend days just browsing among the showcases, I knew. And if I did, the more unpleasant things here must fade into a background that I would come to accept almost without noticing.

For the first time I felt as though I could belong at Glamis. Walking, I imagined myself learning the romantic secrets of the precious things stored here. I would understand better Uncle John's involvement with his artifacts, because I could hardly wait now to examine the contents of those showcases, catalog in hand. I walked faster. The entrance door of the chamber was just ahead.

The doors were massive, but the handle turned. It took all my strength to push one of the heavy doors inward. Flustered from the effort, I stared around curiously. Steps led down into a windowless stone torture chamber, reminding me that the original torture chamber for convenience would've been part of a complex of prison dungeons beneath the Spanish castle. The chamber had neither windows nor exit doors, other than the doors at the entrance. But I could see barred alcoves in the walls down there that must have been a part of the cruel punishment inflicted on those who displeased the church's Grand Inquisitor or the castellan.

I could see into these alcove c⸱⸱⸱ ⸱⸱⸱ w⸱⸱ h a person must squat continually, never able to stand or to straighten cramped limbs. Others were so confined that the prisoner must stand continually, unable to bend his knees. My curiosity prompted me to stare around at the barred alcoves, two to each of the four walls, and each one so cunningly constructed as to inflict painful cramps upon a different set of muscles or joints. Yet these cells, I knew, were as nothing compared to the instruments displayed down there. There would be racks to tear the prisoner's limbs from his body. Iron boots that tightened as a screw was turned slowly until the foot was crushed to pulp.

They lined the walls, these instruments of cruelty,

Somewhere through the numbness of terror I heard a door open, and Ralph's voice called abruptly, "Tracey, have you found Ivan? Tracey, where are you?"

Ivan had been closer to me than I thought. I heard him move stealthily, so close to the cloth hiding me that I gasped instinctively.

"I'm coming, Ralph!" It was strange the way he called back to Ralph, like someone waking from dreaming, someone suddenly much more adult. "I'm checking onyx beads in Fifteen C."

"Where's Tracy? Did a girl tell you I wanted you?"

"Yes. I think she went to the office to wait for Sandra. Sandra isn't here yet."

"Sandra's coming now, I phoned the house to hurry her along. And you'd better get in here and do some work. Uncle John phoned. He's coming some earlier than we expected, and we'd better have something done before he gets here."

"I said I'm coming."

I had been about to leap up and run, desperately. But unexpectedly I was finding reassurance in what they were saying. Ralph muttered something, and the door closed impatiently. I began to quake again. Ralph was gone, and now it was too late to run away. And Ivan was still there.

"I know you're there," he whispered so close I felt he had only to reach out to touch me. "Why are you shaking the cloth? Are you laughing at me?"

"No," I muttered. "Of course not."

"You'd *better not*!" he said in a small boy's threatening tone. "And you'd better not let them catch you hiding there either, you hear me? Nobody is allowed to play in here."

To *play*? I shuddered. "I . . . didn't know that," I muttered sickly, playing out his charade.

"Well, you know now!" he whispered back. "You

might break something they could never replace, no matter how much money Uncle John has. So you watch out! Promise?"

"I promise!" I would have promised anything to be rid of him at that moment, with just a woolen cloth between us.

"What's your name? Tracey, like he said?"

"Yes, Tracey."

"Come on, then, Tracey. I'll help you out of there before they see you."

"No!" I gasped. "I can get out myself. Just go away, and I promise I won't break anything, or let anyone see me. I . . ."

"Quickly! Sandra's coming in. Get up before she sees us here."

I sensed him looming over me and tried to hide my face, but his hands gripped my arms, helping me up, strong but surprisingly gentle. Seeming different hands from those that had torn at me in the railroad yard. I was being guided around the woven cloth and between the figures, his hands helping me, for my knees trembled and gave beneath my weight.

I was in the passage between the showcases then, my hand on one seeking support while he stared at me, and I saw his face for the first time. I could not look away again, because it fascinated me.

"Don't be frightened, Tracey," he whispered. "I won't tell anyone what you did. I wouldn't want them to get mad at *you*."

"Thank you, Ivan," I murmured, and watched him turn and hurry toward the workshop. He glanced back from the door, and I managed to smile at him before he went inside.

My strength came back, and with it my composure. But I could still see Ivan's face with my mind as I walked toward the office where Sandra Craig was just opening the door.

It was the smooth, untroubled face of a boy I had seen. A handsome boy, a boy you might expect to see in a church choir, with innocence masking the hidden mischief beneath. Perhaps that deformed man's body accentuated the way Ivan Brunier looked.

How could a man who had attempted to murder me horribly look like that?

Chapter EIGHT

In Sandra Craig's company I learned more about the chamber in an hour than my own limited knowledge on the subject of torture could have discovered in a week. She shuddered with me as she described the functions of the horrible devices we looked at. Principal among these were the three large machines that stood in line in the center of the chamber not far from the fire. The rack I already understood. The wheel seemed to me to serve much the same purpose of stretching the body, until I realized that it also bent the bones and broke them as the strain increased, dragging the body backward into a circle. The third machine, Sandra told me, was called the "scavenger's daughter." It compressed the body into a solid ball of flesh and bone—slowly, as all these fiendish machines were designed to work.

There were leather, multithonged whips, their tips lead balls to bruise and burst the flesh, or barbed hooks to tear away living strips of flesh from the bone like the hooked teeth of voracious sharks. The instruments of crucifixion and mutilation and slow hanging were there, the iron plates and specially designed probes that heated red roasted the flesh, blinded, or burned out the body's orifices. All the diabolic apparatus of question or punishment that cruelty and perversion could suggest were here in the torture chamber.

Even the alcoves in which prisoners were tormented while they awaited worse torture—burning or the headman's ax—attacked my shuddering imagination more when seen closely than they had when from the door above I had called Ivan from one of them. No two cells I saw now were alike. In some the confined space twisted the body left, in others to the right. One leaned the upright body backward, another forward. In none was it possible to relax, to lie or sit or stand erect.

We had stopped at the alcove cell from which I saw Ivan Brunier emerge. I was tempted to tell Sandra about that, but decided against it. Like her brother Ralph, she seemed nicer to me this morning, but I remembered my promise to Ivan not to inform on him to the others. Ivan hadn't related that promise to his being in the cell, because he didn't know I'd seen him there. But I still felt bound by it. To me, a promise was not made to be broken. I stared into the cell, wondering why I hadn't noticed Ivan in there earlier than I had. Lord knows, Ivan was big enough to see.

"That's about it," Sandra said. "Except for the accessories, as we call instruments of torture not designed to be fatal. They're on the far wall on pegs, anytime you have to check them. There are pincers for pulling out teeth, fingernails, or toenails; screws and other pressure things for breaking lesser bones; the iron boot, of course, which when screwed tight leaves the victim with a clubfoot."

I shuddered. "I think I've seen enough!"

She glanced at me. "Just so long as you can find things when you have to, Tracey," she said. "When Uncle John sends one of us for something in here, he wants it in a hurry. He's like that."

"The exhibits are numbered, and the numbers correspond with the cards and the catalog," I said. "I could find anything he wanted in here right now, if I had to. I'm not a fool, Sandra."

She gave me an odd glance. "No, you're not. You're smart, Tracey. Perhaps too smart for your own good. Okay, we'll go upstairs. The clothing of the executioner and his assistant are replicas. So is the yellow robe of the penitent heretic worn on the way to burning at the stake."

"Nobody was considered innocent until they were found guilty in those days," I said grimly as we moved toward the steps.

She smiled. "That phrase hadn't been invented, Tracey," she said. "To be accused was to be guilty. The purpose of these instruments was mostly to force confession, whether the victim was guilty or not. And since execution was the penalty for most crimes in the Middle Ages, once they confessed, they were summarily burned, or hanged, or beheaded. Execution, and sometimes torture, was considered a form of entertainment by those at whose orders it was inflicted."

We had reached the top of the steps, and she waited while I closed the heavy doors.

"Since you learn so quickly," she said, "you are on your own from here on in. I've other things to do. This afternoon, when Uncle John's here, I'll show you how the cataloging is done. I have some catching up to do before then. Okay?"

I nodded. I'd decided earlier I'd sooner do my checking alone here in the main section. "It isn't going to take me all day. If I can help you catch up, all you have to do is ask."

She studied me for a moment. "Thanks . . . but I'm not very good at asking favors."

"Have it your way," I said. "I can find other ways of passing the time."

"You could take another walk in the old railroad yard," she suggested sarcastically. "Peter McDonald might find you there again."

It didn't seem worth answering, but she had annoyed me. She had welcomed me at first as a companion of her age and sex, but now she resented me, and showed it. We seemed to rub each other the wrong way every time we met. I conceded it wasn't all her fault. We were just incompatible. I had passed two showcases without really knowing what I looked at. I went back and started again. It was quite simple, really, I found, now that I could concentrate. The showcases were lettered, the exhibits numbered. It was just a matter of following the order from A to Z. But it would be easier still if I made myself a map of the museum. Until I memorized the different categories and where they were, a map showing the passages and the codes of the showcases and sections would enable me to walk directly to whatever I wanted, provided it was listed in the catalog.

I began making the notes for my sketch, and quickly forgot Sandra's inexplicable moods. I was halfway through the passages when an old rumbling sound startled me, and I looked up. The chauffeur in his shirt-sleeves was pushing a four-wheeled trolley loaded with small boxes into the museum. He saw me staring as he pushed his load toward the workshop around the wide outer passage that followed the walls of the main section. Watching me over the showcase as he approached, he said cheerfully, "Good morning, Miss Craig. Brought you all some more work. Is Miss Sandra in the workshop?"

"Good morning," I smiled. "No, she's working in the office." I hesitated. "You're the chauffeur, aren't you? I don't know your name?"

"It's Garrick, Miss Craig. Paul Garrick," he said. "Anytime you want a car, all you have to do is ask Mrs. Brunier, and I bring it to the entrance for you."

"Thank you, Paul," I said. "I'll remember."

Peter McDonald had told me that too, I remembered. Peter had said Paul Garrick worked for his father, and that I could trust Paul. I watched him push the heavy trolley around to the workshop, a sturdy man of forty, with dark hair graying at the temples, and a friendly smile. He didn't look back. He reached the workshop door and knocked, and presently Ralph Craig opened it for him and he went inside.

I found it difficult to go back to my notes. Paul Garrick had made himself known to me, as Peter had said he would. And Peter was right; he did seem the kind of man who might help me if I needed help.

I felt better for that. He came back again almost at once without the trolley, but he passed by without looking at me and went back out the museum entrance. I shrugged and returned to my notes. I was just finishing them when I heard Sandra coming from the office. She was frowning, and carried a sheaf of papers in her hand.

She glanced curiously at my notebook. "What on earth are you doing? Listing everything isn't going to help you! They're already listed in the catalog," she said. "You're wasting your time."

"*I* don't think so," I retorted. "I'm making a map of the museum showing the code marking of each show-case and section. That way, if Uncle John wants something in, say, code letter C, I can walk straight to the showcase, or the wall section, find the exhibit number, and that's it. Most museums have a map showing where the different sections are, printed in the back of their catalog. I'll paste mine in, and it will save me problems until I memorize where everything is."

She frowned, considering. "You've got something there. I know it all by heart, but every now and then when Uncle John flusters me, I get a blind spot and can't for the life of me remember where the thing he wants is. You wouldn't like to make a carbon copy of your map for *me* while you're at it, would you?"

I was tempted to remind her of her hang-up about asking favors, but a carbon copy wasn't much trouble, and anything that might relieve the tension between us seemed worthwhile. I nodded. "Okay. I'll even run off a few copies if you have a duplicator."

"There's one in the office."

"I'll need paper."

"In the cupboard. All sizes." She glanced down at the papers in her hand. "You can use Ralph's desk to sketch. It's the one near the window. I have to check these invoices with him, so you can answer the phone if it rings while you're there. Anything you can't handle, just tell them to hold the line while you fetch me. I could be half an hour in the workshop with these."

"Okay, I'll do that," I promised.

"Thanks, Tracey," she said; her smile was involuntary as she turned and hurried away to the workshop.

I stared after Sandra, frowning, wondering what it was that made her the way she was with me. Here we were two girls of the same age in this unfriendly place—and no real communication between us. It was as though she *wanted* to like me, but something, some influence she could not control, prevented her. I decided, sighing, that the obstacle between us had to be Uncle John's money. I was beginning to think we might all be better off without it, if this was the way it made people behave.

Even Uncle John Craig.

I made the last entry and closed my notebook, my mind going back to the proposed map of the museum I must draw. I decided it had better be good, now that I was committed to giving a copy to Sandra and had involved myself in running off other copies for other people, perhaps for the rest of my relatives here at Craig Glamis.

The office door was almost closed, no doubt in the position Sandra had happened to leave it in. I pushed it open unceremoniously, and gasped in fright. Some-one, a man wearing dark trousers and a white shirt with the sleeves rolled up, had started up nervously from behind the desk near the window, the desk Sandra had told me belonged to Ralph.

He shook his head and grinned at me. "You shouldn't frighten a guy that way, Miss Craig!" he said accusingly. "Particularly when we're dealing with people like those involved here."

I let my breath sigh out in relief. That was the Glamis chauffeur, Mr. McDonald's assistant, Paul Garrick, standing guiltily behind Ralph Craig's desk, with the drawers still open, as though he had been searching for something there as I came in. I shook my head.

"I thought I saw you go," I said. "What are you doing at Ralph Craig's desk?"

He grinned at me. "I came back as soon as I was sure Sandra Craig had left the office," he said. "As for what I'm doing—the easiest way would be to say I was doing my job. You know what that is. Peter told you. I'm investigating what you might call unusual hap-penings at Craig Glamis. But just between you and me, I hoped someone had left a key to the museum in one of these drawers. He hasn't. So I'd better close them and get the hell out of here again before some-one else comes in and catches me the way you just did."

"Why do you want a key, Paul?" I asked, closing the door the way he had had it before I came burst-ing in.

"To get in, of course," he said. "And preferably tonight. But I'm out of luck. There's no key in here. I don't suppose you have one?"

"I haven't even started working here yet. I'm just . . . getting to know my way about among the exhibits."

He nodded and went cat-footed to the door to peer out, listening. "They're all still in the workshop," he said with satisfaction.

"Sandra said she could be half an hour away. She asked me to take phone messages for her. You've plenty of time, Paul."

"Then I'll take a look in Sandra's desk, before she changes her mind and comes back," he said in a low voice. "I never did trust that bird. Anytime Sandra Craig tells you something, she means something different, in my experience of her."

"If you start going through Sandra's desk, she'll know," I told him warningly. "Women are like that. One thing out of place, and she'll blame me. Besides, I can save you the trouble. Sandra doesn't have a key. There are only two keys. Ralph has one, and my uncle has the other. Ralph mentioned this when someone was in here the other night, and he couldn't understand how they got in. Ralph carries his museum key in a key wallet. I don't know about Uncle John, because I haven't seen him open the door yet."

He frowned. "Someone was in here at night? You're sure?"

"Ralph said so. He told Uncle John, but by the time they looked for the light, it was gone. Ralph said Uncle John didn't seem disturbed about it. He said my uncle acted as though he knew who it was all the time, and wasn't frightened of anything being stolen. I think I know *why*, Paul."

He stared at me, frowning. "You *do*?"

I nodded. "I saw a light in here too, from my bedroom window. It was around midnight. I saw it clearly. Someone switched a light on in the torture chamber. I saw them walk past the light; then they switched it off quickly. It wasn't on for more than a few seconds."

"You couldn't recognize the person, of course?" he said, frowning. "Not at that distance? Not in one quick glimpse?"

"Probably not," I said. "If I hadn't seen him before that, and again since. And remember, I saw him in silhouette against the light."

He grinned wryly and shook his head. "I'm in the wrong game!" he said admiringly. "Would you mind saying that again slowly?"

"I saw the same person up in the old railroad yard. He was moving a whole line of cars."

He scowled. "Oh, come on, Miss Craig! Nobody could do that. One car perhaps, the one that almost killed Mr. McDonald and you. He was able to move that only because he had it and the switch well greased in preparation. I discovered that the same day it happened. It proved you *had* seen someone push the car, as you told Mr. McDonald and Peter. But we didn't confirm that with you, because Peter didn't want you involved deeper than you already were."

"How much more involved can anyone get than having someone try to kill you?" I demanded indignantly.

He grinned and shook his head. "Peter meant you'd be in more immediate danger if the guy thought you could recognize him. A threat like that must only make him more desperate to remove the source of danger to himself as quickly and as permanently as possible. You realize that?"

"I suppose so, but—"

"As it was, he wouldn't expect you to be able to identify him, even if he saw you staring up the hill

at him. The distance is too great," he said. "Now, tell
me about the third time. Was this when you fainted
and Peter brought you back to the house from the
railroad yards?"

He was thinking I wasn't a very satisfactory witness
if he needed one, I knew. But at least he wasn't like
Peter. *He* listened to me.

"It was," I said. I told him what happened, living
my moment of terror again as I got myself hooked
and was caught and broke away, while he listened silently, frowning.

"When he was so close to you, it was a pity you
couldn't see him," he muttered.

"I couldn't turn to look, even if I hadn't been too
scared. I was stuck fast in there. All I could think
about was getting away," I said.

"That's understandable."

"But that man *was* the same one I saw in the museum the other night," I said triumphantly. "He moved
in the same way. Everything about him was the same."

"The same man who tried to kill you with a railroad car?"

I hesitated, considering that.

"So you're not sure," he persisted, watching my face.

"No, I'm not," I admitted. "I don't think this was
the same man. I have the impression that the man
who sent the runaway car down the hill at us was big-
ger, and . . . somehow different. There was nothing
unusual about him. He . . . well, he was just like any
other man."

"Which doesn't help me," he said ruefully.

"But I *know* the other one," I said. "I saw him
again this morning. He moves exactly the way he did
in here that night. He moves the same way the man
did who chased me in the railroad yard. And in profile each time he was the same. *Unusual!*"

He stared at me, frowning. "*Unusual*, Miss Craig?"

"It was *Ivan*," I said. "Ivan is a hunchback. When I saw him in here this morning and realized that, it scared me. I tried to hide from him, I was so frightened. When he found me, he said, 'You're the girl who got hooked between the cars. Wait for me. Don't run away again."

"Ivan Brunier?" he said slowly. "That figures better than you know, Miss Craig."

"But now that I've seen Ivan and talked to him, he doesn't frighten me anymore. I can't believe Ivan would push that other car down the hill intending to . . . to kill Mr. McDonald and me. He's like a playful boy."

He nodded. "And you say Ivan said you were the girl who got hooked between the cars? When he came up behind you and tugged at your clothes, could he have been trying to release you?"

I stared at him. "I never thought of it that way before, but it's possible. He was tugging and I was scared and struggling like a mad thing. When he tore the cloth, I seemed to break away from him, but I suppose it could have been that he . . . just let me go. I didn't wait to see—I got up and ran."

"Did he run after you?"

"I could hear him running on the other side of the line of cars. He was mumbling something, but I was too scared to hear."

"When he heard you call to Peter for help, he stopped at once?"

"Yes, he did."

"Ivan wouldn't want to be seen there, Miss Craig," he said thoughtfully. "He's forbidden to go outside the grounds. The gardeners have orders not to let him through the gates unless his mother or one of the Craigs is with him."

"Why?" I demanded. "They've no right to do that

to him! He's not *insane*. Ralph says he can do the most delicate restoration work on the artifacts, work a lot of scientists couldn't do."

"He has memory lapses," he said, glancing at the door. "Keeping him inside Glamis isn't a punishment, and it isn't designed to protect people from him. It's to protect Ivan from himself. He could wander off up into the hills, fall from the cliffs. Anything. How do you suppose he got into the railroad yards when he couldn't get out the gates, Miss Craig?"

"All I know is that Ivan *was* there. I'm sure of that, even though I didn't see his face. Anytime Ivan tires of the workshop, Ralph says he just disappears to run off and play someplace like a boy let out of school. So why not the old railroad? Anything outside the workshop is a game to him. When I ran from him and hid this morning, he thought *I* was playing too." I remembered something Peter had said. "Paul, can you tell me what you were brought here to investigate?"

"The theft of artifacts," he said. "They disappeared from the museum four months ago, Miss Craig. They haven't been offered to any dealer, and your uncle hasn't claimed insurance. There were pearls and jewelry pieces of that period, daggers and cups inlaid with gold and precious stones. I was called in because your uncle thought, and I agree, that the stuff has never left Glamis."

I stared at him, shocked. "You think Ivan . . .?"

He nodded. "I think Ivan took the stuff and hid it, and perhaps in his excitement he had a memory lapse. Your uncle and his mother both questioned him about it, but he just doesn't seem to have the slightest recollection of anything like that. Yet he might take things like that, bright, gaudy things, and hide them."

"To play with—*not* to steal," I said, coming to Ivan's defense.

He nodded. "I agree. Yet, take the railroad yard. He's been going there for some time. You said he moved a whole line of cars. That seems impossible, but it could be done with a lever and fulcrum, if the axles and wheels were greased. And they have been greased; I checked on that as soon as Peter told me what you said happened."

"Peter didn't believe *me*," I said, remembering.

"He does now," he said grimly. "The thing is, if Ivan keeps going back to the rolling stock in the yard, I believe that sooner or later he'll go back to the artifacts. If he doesn't, then we'll have to presume that someone else took them. Perhaps hoping Ivan would be blamed, and they're waiting as long as they can before selling. And if we believe that, why not believe what you do—that someone else, not Ivan, tried to kill you and almost killed Angus McDonald with you?"

"Which gives us a thief as well as a potential murderer?" I shivered. "And perhaps one of the Craig family? I'd sooner believe poor Ivan did these things. That he took the artifacts to play with, and started the railroad car rolling without intending to *hurt* anyone."

"I'd like to believe that too," he said. "I keep imagining that whole line of railroad cars you mentioned hurtling down the hill and someone in the cut—"

I had been absorbed by our conversation, and I'm sure the same thing had happened to Paul Garrick, because he looked as startled as I felt when someone pushed the partially closed door wide open abruptly and looked in at us. My Uncle Edward stood in the doorway studying us through narrowed amber eyes, and there was no way of knowing how much he'd heard. Uncle Edward was not the man to allow his expression to betray his thoughts.

His strange pale eyes studied my face speculatively.

"When I heard a woman's voice in here, Tracey," he said, "I thought it must be my daughter. Where is Sandra?"

"She's in the workshop, Uncle Edward," I said nervously.

"I'll talk to her there." He looked at Paul Garrick coldly. "Are you working in the office now, Garrick?"

"No, Mr. Craig," Paul Garrick muttered.

"Then I suggest you return to your garages, and get on with the work my brother pays you to do," Uncle Edward said spitefully.

"Yes, Mr. Craig," Paul Garrick said humbly. "I was just going."

I opened my mouth to protest indignantly, but my eyes met those of the chauffeur, and I read a warning there that held me silent.

Uncle Edward's look seemed to say: And that goes for you, too, Tracey Craig.

He closed the door and went away, without any change of expression, or any hint that he had, or had not, heard what we were discussing.

I sighed and went to Ralph's desk and found paper and pens and started on my map of the museum. Working, I wondered if Uncle Edward had been listening outside the door of the office while I talked to the chauffeur. I could imagine Uncle Edward listening at doors. But not pushing railroad cars at people. He was far too indolent for that. And Ralph, with his professed hatred of violence. Could Ralph attempt to kill me? Sandra wasn't the type either, nor did she have the strength for it, any more than I did.

I began to think about Donald, and found that all I knew about him was that I hadn't liked him since he tried to make me drink something I was sure would make me drunk, in some stupid attempt to discredit me with Uncle John. All I knew of Donald was that he ran the Aberfeld office of Craig Investments, and was athletic enough to play golf. I began to think very seriously about my cousin Donald.

We had barely finished lunch, and I was running off a dozen copies of the map on the duplicator when Uncle John came in. I expected to be immediately caught up in the rush of work that both Ralph and Sandra had warned me to expect when Uncle John was around, but in my case today that didn't seem to apply.

True, he asked them a few curt questions and sent Ralph off to the workshop looking anxious. Then he came over to see what I was doing at the duplicator. I did not have to tell him. He picked up a copy and studied it, frowning. He nodded.

"I *like* that. When we have the next catalog printed, Sandra, remind me to reserve space on the back cover for this map. Put Tracey's original sketch away for the blockmakers."

Sandra gave me an unpleasant look, so I said placatively, "I only made a rough map for my own use to help me find any exhibit you wanted, Uncle John. I meant to paste it in the back of my catalog. Sandra saw it and came up with the idea of making other copies. And she's right. Your system for exhibits is so straightforward, it's made for a map like this one."

He nodded. "I'll keep this copy for my own catalog. It's a pity Sandra didn't think of something like this a long time ago. She had plenty of time. Usually I find museum maps a useless jumble of numbers, but this one is explicit. I could walk to any exhibit at once with the help of this map. And that's something even *I* can't do at times."

"Tracey is a clever girl," Sandra said bitterly.

He glanced at her and nodded. "Yes, isn't she? I see you're still wearing that wig, Sandra. I don't know how girls can wear wigs. No wig ever made can reproduce the beauty of a young woman's healthy, natural hair. Look at Tracey's."

Uncle John was adding my map to a sheaf of papers he carried in a folder as Sandra glared at me. I changed my mind about Sandra as that look got me. She *could* commit murder, in my case even by slow torture.

Uncle John straightened with his folder. "I haven't quite made up my mind what I want you to do in here yet, Tracey," he said. "So now that you've oriented yourself with the aid of your map, you can browse or go back to the house, whichever you like."

"I'd like to browse in here, thank you. I'm finding all this even more interesting than I expected," I said eagerly.

"Good. Sandra, bring your notebook to the workshop; we've some checking to do there. . . ." He broke off and groped in a pocket of his jacket. "I almost forgot. Yvonne said there was a message for you, Tracey. You're to call this number. . . ."

He gave it to me and followed Sandra, who was already stalking out with a notebook in her hand, her back one straight, angry line all the way up to the crown of her head. When he was outside, I remembered that Uncle John hadn't told me *how* Yvonne received the message, or *who* it was I was supposed to call. But I needn't have worried, I saw as I unfolded the leaf from a memo pad Yvonne Brunier had scribbled on. I knew that phone number with the Aberfeld code; it was Angus McDonald's.

I had picked up the office phone when I remembered Sandra's voice cutting in the last time I called the McDonald home. Uncle John would have her too busy to eavesdrop right now, but there was still Ralph with a phone on his desk in the workshop that he had only to pick up, while over in the house were Uncle Edward and Aunt Mary. I could imagine them picking up a phone the moment one indicated the outside line was busy. Aunty Mary and Uncle Edward had nothing else to do it seemed to me.

I remembered Uncle John's private phone in his study then, the one line the inquisitive couldn't listen in to. I started to put the phone down, but a thought occurred to me, and I put it to my ear instead. And someone *was* listening in. I could hear heavy, hoarse breathing so plainly that I knew at once who it was. Only my Uncle Edward breathed like that, asthmatically, after hurrying or when excited.

"You really will have to do something about your weight," I said. "Your breathing is beginning to sound quite asthmatic, Uncle Edward."

"What?" he said, startled. "What was that you said? Tracey, you insolent girl!"

I managed to hold my giggle in until the phone was back in place. It didn't matter then, because the workshop was too far away for my amusement to arouse curiosity. The air was crisp and cold outside the museum, and if Uncle John looked for me in the museum, it didn't matter, because he'd said I had a choice there. Paul Garrick was polishing one of the Glamis cars outside the garages. He had a quick eye, that man. He saw me the moment I came out, and gave me a discreet recognition signal with his chamois polisher.

Inside the house I approached the reception room warily, knowing it to be Uncle Edward's favorite haunt. Aunt Mary was listening in on the phone in there, her absolute concentration suggesting she had waited for me to ring again. Uncle Edward was muttering angrily to himself at the corner bar as he poured a Scotch, with his back toward me. The long, wide corridor to the kitchen was empty too. In the study I locked the door with the key Peter had said was always there, and sank gratefully into Uncle John's deep leather chair.

Yvonne Brunier had been in here to take the call that brought my message. The pad the message had come from was beside the phone, with part of the McDonalds' number indented in Yvonne's scrawl on the clean page below the one she had sent me. Sometimes it surprised me how close Yvonne was to Uncle John. She could've been the mistress of Glamis, as my mother once was, rather than its housekeeper.

I sighed and dialed the number, and Angus McDonald answered so quickly he could've been sitting beside it waiting for my call.

"Tracey Craig?" his deep voice asked anxiously.

"You left me a message."

"Your uncle said you were at the museum. Are you calling from there, Tracey?"

I smiled. "It's okay, Mr. McDonald. I'm calling from Uncle John's study. I started to call from the museum, but I heard a third party listening in, so I came here. I've locked myself in the study, and nobody can hear me. Your son, Peter, told me this line is completely private and is the one I should use to call you. Right?"

"My son occasionally shows glimmerings of common sense," he said. "Do you know which one of your sly relatives was listening in just now?"

"Uncle Edward," I said with certainty. "I knew the way he breathed. I told him he should lose some weight because he's almost an asthmatic."

He chuckled. "You told Edward *that*, did you? Edward, eh? I wonder. You're sure it was Edward?"

"He was muttering to himself and pouring a Scotch just now as I passed the reception-room door," I said. "Aunt Mary had taken over the phone in his absence, waiting for me to call again. And, yes, it *was* Uncle

Edward—I heard his voice when I needled him. He called me an insolent girl."

"Well," he said thoughtfully, "it doesn't matter greatly what he thinks of you now, or says about you, for that matter. We're taking you out of there, Peter and I. We decided that last night, in view of some new evidence I found among your father's effects. It was a mistake that you were ever brought here. Your father's mistake—not mine, Tracey. If he'd taken *me* into his confidence, you wouldn't be at Glamis. But no, out of the blue through his brother John, he called on my integrity to force me to advise you. Wrongly, as it turned out, because I had insufficient facts. So I placed your life in danger, and mine with it."

"How could he take you into his confidence when you hated him?" I was growing angry again as I remembered. "You told me that yourself."

" 'Dislike' was the word I used, Tracey," he said. "Don't try to twist the words of an old attorney like me. Others have tried that before you. We're taking you from Glamis, and the sooner the better. You'll not spend another night in that place of treachery if I can help it."

I stared at the phone. "You mean you want me to move from here *today*?" I asked in dismay. Where to? Where could I go? I have nowhere."

"Mrs. McDonald is preparing a room for you," he said. "You're coming to stay with us till we see what happens at Glamis. You'll be safe and welcome here, Tracey Craig. For as long as you please."

"Because you feel responsibility for me? I couldn't do that Mr. McDonald," I protested. "I'm grateful, of course, but you're not . . . not kin of mine."

"Were the Craigs of Glamis, till I brought you here?"

I frowned. "That was different. Something my father ordered me to do, and you advised was best for me."

"Don't rub it in, Tracey," he said ruefully. "We, all three of us, want you here with us now, for both my wife and Peter think, as I do, that there's danger for you at Glamis. When that danger passes, as I believe it will, you can go back. But not before then. How about that, Tracey Craig?"

I stared at the phone for a long moment before I said slowly, "I don't expect you to understand, but suddenly I don't want to leave Glamis, Mr. McDonald. I'm not frightened here as I was. Paul Garrick made himself known to me this morning; maybe that's why. I feel I can get help quickly if I need help now. I've met Ivan Brunier, and he doesn't frighten me anymore, now that I understand him. I know my cousins Sandra and Ralph better. I might not like them, but I could live with them, I think. And there's Uncle John to consider. I . . . feel drawn to him, Mr. McDonald. I like him, and I sense that he's beginning to like me, despite all those years he hated Dad. He paid me a compliment today, about my hair. And he praised something I did for his museum. And that, the museum, is another consideration. Now that I've seen it, I know that I can work in there and like what I'm doing. I mean to do that, starting tomorrow."

"You're a stubborn girl, Tracey!" he growled. "Very well. I can't take you from Glamis against your will, more's the pity, since Henry Craig didn't have the foresight to make *me* your legal guardian. And I can't reason with you, since you're guided by feeling, not by reason. But tell me something—how am I to tell Peter that you prefer the dangers and hostility of Glamis to the hospitality and friendship of the Mc-Donalds? How can I tell him that you reject the things he's planned for you in Aberfeld? That you want no part of us, or him?"

"I didn't say *that*!" I muttered, suddenly confused because somehow he'd brought Peter into it, and that was making me feel guilty. Guilt always made me angry. It was beginning to do that to me now.

"It's what you *mean*," he said grimly.

"I don't see what my decision has to do with Peter," I said indignantly. "Why should it?"

"It's his place to answer that, not mine. I can only tell you what I think," Peter's father said grimly. "A girl like you—a girl become woman—should know better than me whether a man loves her or not."

"*What*?" I said, startled. "He *couldn't*! Peter couldn't—"

"Maybe he can reason with you better than I can, so you think about what I said, Tracey." He could have been threatening me, his voice sounded so severe. "I'm bringing Peter to Glamis tonight with me, for in the light of this new evidence, there are things I must say to your Uncle John, and maybe to others. And if you've one ounce of sense in that pretty head of yours, you'll have your bags packed when we get there."

"This evidence, Mr. McDonald—what is it?" I demanded. "If it was found among my father's papers, I have a right to know what it was."

"That's for your uncle to decide," he said gruffly. "It concerns him as much as it does you."

I heard his phone go down, and sat there with mine still held in my hands, whatever he had found in my father's effects losing importance as I thought about Peter.

Peter couldn't have fallen in love with me. He *couldn't*! Or I with him. Ridiculous! But there *was* this warm feeling I had when he was near me. This feeling of not wanting him to go.

I went slowly up to my room, hearing the mutter of

voices in the reception room as I passed and was seen. Someone, Aunt Mary I think, called to me, but I took no notice. . . .

Chapter NINE

I escaped from the family as quickly as I could when dinner ended. Both Uncle Edward and Donald had been particularly unpleasant at table, and Donald had pressured Ralph into drinking with him both before and during the meal. I'd never seen Ralph drunk before. He usually had only a light wine with dinner or an occasional Scotch with his father. He was half-asleep and slurring his words long before coffee.

I was glad to escape with Sandra and Uncle John, Sandra carrying Ralph's keys to the museum, which she had obtained from him with some difficulty because she still had some invoicing to do. Uncle John had remarked acidly on her unusual industry, adding that if she had felt the same way during the afternoon she wouldn't need to work at night. It had seemed unusual to me too that Sandra should want to work there at night alone. I remembered all the eerie figures and things in there and shuddered involuntarily.

"It must be spooky in there at night, Sandra," I said. "Would you like me to go with you?"

"Why should she?" Uncle John said. "If Sandra hasn't done her work, that's her fault. And she knows as well as I do that dead things from a past age can't hurt anyone."

"I know that, Uncle John," I smiled. "But Sandra is a girl. Logic doesn't come into it when we're scared. Believe me, I know."

Sandra was studying my face, ignoring him. She

said gratefully, "Would you really, Tracey? I'd love you to, but I just couldn't ask."

"Of course I will," I said, trying not to imagine what it would be like in there at night.

Uncle John gave an angry snort and shook his head. "I'm going to the study. Tracey, whether she's finished or not, I want to see you in the study at nine-thirty. The McDonalds are coming here tonight, and the subject we have to discuss concerns you—so you be there."

I frowned, remembering how I'd worked on that problem as I saw it all afternoon. I said, "If it concerns my leaving Craig Glamis, Uncle John, I've decided to stay. I'm learning to like it here."

He scowled at me unexpectedly. "It concerns much more than that, Tracey," he said gruffly. "So you be there, or I'll send someone for you at nine-thirty."

"I'll be there," I promised.

He had turned and was walking toward his study, so I shrugged and followed Sandra.

"What was all that about?" she demanded curiously.

"The McDonalds want me to leave Glamis, because of the things that happened to me," I said. "I think that's what it's really about tonight. I thought it over, and decided against running away. I'm not frightened anymore Sandra."

"He said it was more than that." Her gray eyes probed, with more than just curiosity, it seemed to me. "If he says that, it is."

"I don't know of anything else."

"Oh, come on, Tracey," she said. "The trouble with you is you don't *want* to trust any of us. If you can't turn to one of your own family, who can you turn to? The McDonalds? They're not your kin."

She opened the door and waited for me to pass through. It was very dark outside, I saw. The sky was full of thick, dark clouds, the moon and stars hidden.

"You've forgotten that until I was brought here by Mr. McDonald, so far as I knew, I had no family."

"So there is something else," she said. "Something Angus McDonald told you that you don't want us to know." She shook her head. "It's all right, Tracey, you don't have to tell me—if you don't trust me. . . ."

I frowned and hunched my shoulders in their thin dress against a wind chilling me after the warmth of the dining room with its glowing fire. It didn't seem all that important when I thought back to what Angus McDonald had warned me about. Against the chance to win the friendship of a girl cousin of my own age, it didn't seem very important at all.

I said slowly, "I don't *know* of any other reason why the McDonalds are coming here tonight to see Uncle John. Mr. McDonald wanted me to leave here tonight because he felt that danger for me had increased."

"Why?" she demanded, leaning with me into the wind.

"Because of something, some paper or papers I think, that he'd found among my father's effects."

"A . . . birth certificate?" she asked sharply.

I smiled. "I don't know what it was he found. But I don't see how any birth certificate of my father's or my mother's or mine could increase *my* danger. A birth certificate? What put that into your head?"

"I don't know. Maybe, then, it was a will?"

"He had nothing to leave," I said.

"Damnit!" she said disgustedly. "I'm no good at riddles! Come on, let's get out of this wind!"

She started off running across the lawns between the wind-distorted shapes of giant chessmen shrubs. Not wanting to be left alone, I ran after her. I stumbled and almost fell as the grassy lawn became a gravel drive. The museum was just ahead. She had stopped near the entrance, waiting for me, her breath puffing out from our running, as mine was. I followed her inside gratefully, as she threw a switch and light flooded the building.

"What is there to do, Sandra? You said invoicing, I think?"

She glanced at me and smiled. "I'll show you, Tracey. First, though, I've a phone call to make; then we have some checking to do in the chamber."

"In *there*?" If I'd known I was letting myself in for *that*, I mightn't have come. "Yuk!" I said.

"Oh, it won't take long," she reassured me. "Would you like to take your notebook and wait for me there? The phone call is to my boyfriend, so . . . do you mind?"

I smiled. "I didn't know you had one." I added hastily, "Not that boys anywhere wouldn't run after a girl as pretty as you!" I recovered my notebook and went out, but though I stopped near the closed doors of the chamber, Sandra had misjudged the acoustics of the museum, for I could still hear her voice plainly with the office door open.

"Yes," she was saying. "Tracey's here with me, darling. No, it can't wait. We're going to have to do it now. No! *Now*, I said. Look, I don't know where Ivan is, and I don't *care*. Tonight they're going to know as much as we do, if we just sit around and wait. Do you want that? Neither do I. I'm not going to like it any more than you are, but that doesn't mean I won't see it through."

I moved farther away, guiltily, but needn't have bothered. Sandra was coming from the office carrying her keys, a bright-eyed, smiling Sandra I hadn't seen before. But her expression changed, becoming her usual sullen self again as she came up.

"I told him you were helping me, and it wouldn't

take long," she said. "So let's hurry it up, shall we? I want you to go down and list the new stuff Uncle John put there. I'll give you the corresponding number for the exhibit from up here. Okay?"

"Okay," I muttered, beginning to grow doubtful at the thought of being alone down there. "I didn't know you kept those doors locked. Why?"

"Why?" She frowned, unlocking the heavy doors. "Oh, that's just a bug Ralph got about seeing lights down here at night. He's odd. He got the idea Ivan was coming here, getting in through the chamber, although there's no way in except through this door. He started locking these doors nights."

"Did the lights stop?" I asked, thinking of my own experience, as I helped her pull the doors back.

"I wouldn't know. I've never seen them," she said disdainfully. "Well, are you going to help me or not?" She seemed to be becoming impatient.

"Won't you need your office index cards to give me the new numbers?" I wasn't going to wait alone in that spooky place below us while she got them, if she hadn't brought them with her.

"Damnit," she said frowning. "I forgot the cards. I'll get them. Those are the new artifacts along the wall. Ralph will exhibit them tomorrow morning first thing. That's why we have to write the numbers on tonight."

I had turned instinctively to search for them, seeing them against the far wall.

She gave a spiteful cry and pushed me then as hard as she could. One second I stood at the top of the stone steps, the next I was plunging head-first downward, missing the first steps because of the force of the shove she had given me. A scream of fright that started in my throat ended in a gasp of pain as I hit the stone edges of the steps. Yet somehow it seemed I twisted or was thrown sideways in falling, and started rolling down, trying to stop myself but unable to until I reached the stone floor and stopped there, strangling for breath I could not find to fill my agonized lungs.

Even then I could not believe that it had been deliberate. Among my gasping cries I kept appealing to Sandra for help. It would be impossible to fall like that and not be injured, and the way I felt as the pain came from my injuries and I fought for breath, I was sure that I was dying.

"Sandra!" I pleaded in hoarse gasps. "Help . . . me!"

I saw blood running down the backs of the hands I was trying to force myself upright with then, and began to feel the nausea that comes before fainting, while sweat beaded coldly on my forehead and upper lip. In desperation I tried to sit up, and distinctly then above me at the top of the steps I heard Sandra Craig laugh softly. The doors closed, and I heard the lock click.

"*Sandra*!" The shock brought my breath back, for I screamed her name in terror, and again and again, deafening myself until I remembered suddenly that the original of these walls were designed to deaden the screams of victims in far worse travail than mine. I hitched myself backward painfully to the bottom step and dragged myself onto it, so that, sitting, I faced the chamber, with my back to the steps. My enemy was there behind me, I knew now. Sandra Craig, who had sent me hurtling down these steps to lock me in this place of medieval terror, this chamber of tortures and unspeakable things that had horrified me from the start.

But now in the utter silence that followed my screaming I feared the room before me much more than I did Sandra. I stared around in terror at the group of sadistic wax dummies in the far corner, the implements of excruciating torture with which experts had wrung confessions of heresy from the bravest

Christian men. The executioner and his assistants stared back at me as intently, one assistant gripping a whip with iron-tipped thongs in one waxen hand, the other in classic pose leaning slightly on his master's great ax.

The executioner wore a white cross on the breast of his black robe, and beneath the hood, his face was masked in black. His eyes glittered, staring across the room at me; his hands, as he posed with uncompromising folded arms, were gloved in the same black.

I shuddered and looked away. I tried to remind myself of what Uncle John had said. These dead things from a distant past had no power to harm me. It was the living I should fear. And as I thought of that, I began to shiver with fright, with Sandra's phone conversation with her "boyfriend" suddenly taking a different image. It had seemed to me innocent then, the conversation of two lovers. But not now.

Sandra had trapped me here. She had told whoever it was that she had me here. And she had said. "We're going to have to do it now. . . . Tonight they're going to know as much as we do, if we just sit around and wait." And she had told him, perhaps when he protested: "I'm not going to like it any more than you are, but that doesn't mean I won't see it through."

I shuddered. It didn't matter whether the man she spoke to was really her boyfriend or her father or her brother. They couldn't leave me locked in here. They had to do something about me quickly. I would be missed at nine-thirty, and Sandra knew it.

Sandra had gone through with her part as she promised. Now it was *his* turn. *And his task was to kill me!*

I gasped and dragged myself around to stare up at the closed doors in dismay. Anytime now, those doors would open, and he would come for me, my murderer. Or perhaps there would be two of them? Or three?

I remembered suddenly how Donald had been forcing drinks on Ralph, who hated violence. . . .

I had to find somewhere to hide in here. I had to! It was my only chance. I stared around frantically with all kinds of wild ideas born of desperation taking shape in my mind. Perhaps I could hide beneath the rack? Or the wheel? Or take the place of one of those horrible figures, or make an extra one by taking robes from their places. . . .

But even as I worried at it, I knew that nothing like that could possibly save me. Sandra knew the only way out of here was through those doors she had locked on me. No matter where I hid in this horrible place, they must find me, knowing I must still be in here.

Perhaps if I could elude them for a little while, and scream loudly enough when the doors opened, someone in the house might hear and help me. I was good at screaming, I had discovered, and when they came for me, I would be better still, I was sure. There must be some weapon in here I could use. I thought of the torturer's whip suddenly, and struggled to my feet. For a moment the pain in my legs took all my attention while I tried them gingerly. But I could stand on them, so I'd walk if it killed me.

My eyes searched for the whip in the hand of the executioner's assistant, and I froze in sudden horror, too shocked to scream or cry out.

The executioner was unfolding his arms!

My stomach turned over sickly. My murderer did not have to come from the outside. I had been wrong about that. He was already in here with me. He had been standing there watching me, allowing me to recover until in his own chosen time he came for me. And he was coming for me now. I began to edge away from the steps, going left. There were no weapons there to help me, just the barred alcoves, but at least I felt that for a little while I was keeping away from him.

He was coming toward me around the rack, moving as slowly as I was, and as he moved now, he began to mutter to himself, while the hair on the back of my neck prickled and my heart thumped in sick fright. I caught my name and Sandra's muffled behind the mask, though what he said, in my present state, I could not understand. My back struck the stone wall then beyond the steps, and I could go no farther. And suddenly he was coming faster, his hands reaching up to the hood of his macabre gown.

I opened my mouth and screamed, and screamed again, while my eyes closed as he tore at his robe as though seeking the weapon for my murder. My last hopeless shriek faded to whimpering, and I felt my knees begin to buckle as he reached me and seized my arm and began to shake me.

"Tracey, be quiet! Please, Tracey! You scare me when you yell like that! You mustn't, or they'll hear, and then there'll be trouble for us both."

Slowly, through the haze bemusing my hysterical mind, the words and the voice began to penetrate. My whimpering died, and I sagged in his hands, shaking. He held me propped against the stone wall while he pleaded with me to be quiet, telling me that he hadn't meant to scare me, that he was only playing.

I opened my eyes slowly. He had pulled back the hood of the robe, and the mask was gone, and the scared little boy's face was that of Ivan Brunier, looking incongruous in his executioner's robe spread wide by his hunched back and wide shoulders.

I said disbelievingly, "Ivan? *Ivan!*"

"I told you not to play in here," he said, scolding me now in his relief that I had quietened. "She saw you. Isn't that why Sandra locked you in? But she had no right to hurt you like that. I saw her push you down the steps. There's blood on your clothes, and you're all mussed up. You'll catch it when your uncle sees you."

I stared at him, clutching at straws suddenly. "She locked us *both* in here, Ivan. You're locked in too, you know. And when they find you in here with me, you'll catch it too from your mother, won't you?"

He squirmed uneasily and released me, frowning. "They can't catch me. I'll run away." But he glanced uneasily up at the closed doors, and it sounded like bravado when he added, "They don't scare *me* any!"

"They scare *me*," I said. "Look . . ." I showed him the blood on the back of my hands, and the torn material of the frock, with more blood crusted on my arm visible through the tear. It made me feel sick just looking at it. I whimpered with pain as he poked at it curiously.

"Does it hurt, Tracey?" he muttered sympathetically.

"Of course it hurts, Ivan!" I muttered indignantly. "How would you like to have it? And it's not only there, I'm hurt all over. And she'll hurt me again when she comes back. There will be men with her this time. They'll kill both of us if they catch us in here!" I looked at him, pleading now. "Ivan, I'm scared! Please? Help me get away from them to Uncle John? He won't let them hurt us."

He avoided my eyes. "They don't scare me."

"No, they don't, because *you* know a way out of here," I said bitterly. "And don't lie about it to me. *I know you do!*"

"I don't know what you're talking about, Tracey," he mumbled uneasily.

"I saw you in here one night, from my bedroom window," I accused. "But I didn't tell anyone that. I didn't get you into trouble, did I? So why don't you trust me now, Ivan? And just now, you were in here before Sandra brought me in here and pushed me down the steps, and you didn't get in through the door then, either. Help me, Ivan. I'm your friend."

He moved away from me and wriggled his massive shoulders uncertainly. "I can't take you with me," he muttered. "You want to find all my secret things, and I won't let you." He frowned. "Besides, it's dark in there, and you're a girl. You'd be scared silly."

"I'll be more scared if you leave me here!" I said with certainty. I broke off, listening in terror. Somewhere distantly I'd heard a faint sound. Like the closing of a door. He heard it too, for I saw fright come into his brown eyes abruptly. "Ivan, they're coming!" I gasped in terror.

I grabbed for him, anything to keep him here with me, but he was too quick for me. I missed his arm, and he was gone, running to the barred alcove I had seen him emerge from one morning. I tried to follow him but cried out in agony at the pain in my right ankle. I looked down, and even in the time since Sandra had imprisoned me here it had doubled in size and was turning blue-black. I'd broken it, I was sure. I couldn't bear my weight on it.

"Ivan, *help me*!" I called to him.

He took no notice. He had gone down on his knees and was raising the iron-bar grille. He bent to crawl beneath it into that awkward, confined space intended only to cramp and torture the muscles and joints.

"Ivan!" I screamed. "I can't walk! My ankle's broken! She broke it."

With the palms of his hands he was pushing one of the huge stones at the back of the tiny cell, and while I watched disbelievingly, it began to move, turning sideways as though on an axle, and I saw that the stone itself was not square as I expected, but had been shaved away to a thickness of only a few inches.

"Come on!" he called over his shoulder. "Hurry, Tracey!"

I was trying to make it, hopping. It hurt my other leg, and I fell. I started crawling, groaning with each movement. I was close to the cell before he had the stone fully turned and gave me his attention.

"Be quick!" he ordered. "If we don't get it shut before they come into the chamber, they'll know where we are."

I gritted my teeth against the pain, trying to ignore it, to put every effort into moving toward what I knew was the difference between life and death.

Instinctively, I suppose, I held out my hand to him, and he reached out under the bars to seize my wrist and pull. I was hauled into the cell with him as unceremoniously as the last wearer of his horrible robe would have dragged the body of a victim away with one of the meat hooks on the walls of the torture chamber behind me.

"I'll crawl through," he muttered, "and pull you after me."

But suppose he didn't? my terror suggested. Suppose he just closed the stone door and kept right on going? It wasn't Ivan they wanted to kill, it was *me*.

I had forced my head and shoulders past him into the space between the stone wall and his secret door before he could turn.

"What are you doing?" he muttered in angry surprise. "I told you—"

"Quick! They're coming. You push, and I'll wriggle, and . . ."

Beside me he turned awkwardly and got one hand on me from behind and began to push. I moved a few inches and stuck tight. Inside was thick darkness now as my body filled the space. I reached out and could feel nothing ahead, or below me. Regretting my impulse to escape this way, I tried as desperately now to wriggle back again before I pitched head-first into what seemed to me like a bottomless black pit.

"Tracey, stop it!" he grunted. "What are you doing?"

I cried out in pain and fear as I felt big hands grip my legs just above the knees. He heaved them, and I screamed and was leaving the torture chamber of Uncle John's museum like a cork from a champagne bottle. I fell heavily, my hands reacting instinctively, only partly breaking my fall onto a stone floor.

As I sat up in terror, the light streaming through from the torture chamber blinded me temporarily, before Ivan's head and shoulders moving in blacked out the light. Feeling blindly and with my heart thudding, I groped my way farther away before he fell on me. I came up against another stone wall, damp, smelling of mildew and decay. I leaned against it in pain and exhaustion. Beside me, Ivan grunted. I saw him stand and seize the revolving stone. It began to turn back in slowly, cutting off the light.

Darkness came. A thick, impenetrable darkness such as I had never experienced before. From it, like a disembodied spirit, Ivan's voice whispered nervously, "Come on, Tracey! We can't stay *here*. I saw them opening the doors as I closed the stone. They could hear us in here."

"Go *where* then?" I whispered, trembling. "It's too dark to move! Don't you have a light?"

"Not here, I don't," he said. "But I know the way, so there's nothing for you to get scared about. I thought you were brave."

I was trying to get up when out of the black nothing all about me, his hand found my arm and jerked me upright. "Who, me?" I quavered. "Where are we? What is this place we're in?"

"We're inside the wall of Glamis. In a passage in the wall's base."

My hopes rose. "Then . . . can we follow it around and get out somewhere near enough to the house for me to get there?"

"There's no way," he said. "It only goes as far as the railroad and the mine. Do you want to go to the railroad? I'll give you a ride—"

"No thanks, Ivan," I said hastily. "I hurt too much. I just want to get to Uncle John. Dr. McDonald is with him. I know Peter will help me."

Thought of Peter started my tears flowing; I didn't know why. I cried silently, because as I said it, Ivan told me to shush. I listened with him, trembling.

The stone muted it, but there was no mistaking Sandra's voice as she called to me. "Tracey, come out! We know you're in here. There's no way out. You can't hide from us in here for long, so you might as well come out."

Ivan's hand on my arm startled me as he shook me angrily. "They're going to find my door," he hissed. "And it's all your fault! You made me forget the stone dust on the floor. It always grinds off when the stone's moved. He'll see it and find the door and come after us."

That was what I'd seen Ivan doing in there, I remembered, cleaning away the dust after he'd used the door.

A different voice, a man's voice, said to Sandra, "You'd better be right about this, Sandy! If she got away, we've had it, and all I've risked for you gone for nothing while we rot in a jail."

"I tell you, she can't get out," Sandra said angrily. "Come on, let's find her. And if you don't have the nerve to do it, I will! *I hate her*! Coming here and wrecking something that took us years to build! I wish I'd killed her on the steps. But she's hurt. You saw the blood. She couldn't get far, even if that filthy hunchback knew some secret way out and helped her."

"I told you we should've killed Ivan first," the man said. "But you said no! Okay, let me do this. Go back up the steps so she can't slip past you. If she's in here, I'll find her."

I could feel Ivan's hand trembling on my arm, and he was breathing quickly in fright. "You heard what he said about you?" I whispered.

"It's the man who broke my car!" he breathed. "He ran it down the hill and smashed it up. He's a bad man! But I won't let him get you, Tracey. I'll show you where to hide."

Sandra's voice said abruptly, closer, louder than it had seemed before, "Come here! There's blood in this *cell*! On the floor . . . more on the wall at the back! It's *hers*! It has to be hers!"

Ivan was tugging at my arms suddenly, and like him, I wanted nothing more than to be far from there. But not left alone in this awful place. So I gritted my teeth and kept up with him as best I could, taking hold of part of his robe in a death grip I never meant to loosen, limping, staggering, lurching against first one wall and then the other of that narrow passage, dragging him back each time his impatient fright prompted him to break away. I was hurried through that awful darkness until exhaustion forced me to stop him and stare back. And suddenly the darkness seemed the lesser evil, for far behind us, torchlight blossomed and started in pursuit of us.

The sight of that light coming renewed my will to escape, but my strength was not equal to it. I lost my grip on Ivan's robe, and he forged away from me as I released him, then came back hesitantly.

"Tracey?" he panted. "Come on! *They'll catch us!*"

"I can't!" I gasped from where I had slumped down. "Can't . . . Ivan! You go on! Tell them in the house. Quickly! Tell Uncle John!"

"No!" he muttered. "They'll hurt you again. No . . . I know a place! I'll hide you there."

I was being scooped up suddenly in arms incredibly powerful, cradled against a big chest that thumped with the effort of his run, but not intolerably as mine was thumping, while the boy's mind in that distorted strongman's body mumbled to itself, seeking reassurance from my closeness that suddenly he didn't want to lose.

"Ivan, *stop!*" I gasped.

He had turned and was running with me now, running back toward that pursuing light that seemed so much closer now where it danced on the stone floor and walls of the passage. He stopped abruptly, groping with his left hand along the wall, searching until his fingers encountered what he sought, and he grunted in satisfaction. He was turning then, walking carefully into some place that began at the wall. His foot kicked something that chinked, and he stopped abruptly and put me down.

"They won't find you here," he said confidently. "But you mustn't move, Tracey. You're lying on a rug on a platform of one of the old mine shafts. Its ventilation shaft goes up through the wall above us like a stone chimney, with rungs set in the stone that I can climb and come down in the garden behind Glamis. If you move off the rug while I'm away, you could fall into the shaft, and it goes way down below the sea."

"I won't move!" I shuddered.

"I'll stay with you till they pass. . . ." He broke off

and sank down beside me on the rug. "Shush! They're coming."

There was a change in the darkness, a lessening. Light began to reflect on the wall of the passage seen through a narrow opening. I could hear their breathless voices muttering as they approached. The light strengthened, blindingly after the total darkness, and my heart turned over sickly as it stopped, and Sandra's voice said fiercely, *"Blood!"*

The man's voice said eagerly, "Where?"

The torch steadied, and I gave up hope. *"Here!* Look, there's an opening and . . . *She's in there!"*

The torch had steadied on my face where I ~~lay~~. All I could see was its dazzling light. A second torch appeared, and it too centered on me where I lay too scared to move. But I saw something else now, something that I didn't want to see. It was a man's hand gripping one of the medieval maces from the museum, a malletlike weapon with a short handle and a thong fitted around his wrist.

"Kill her!" Sandra hissed. "There she is! Kill the little bitch *now*. Drag her out here where I can see you do it!"

"Hold this," he said, and gave her the torch. He pushed past her, coming toward me, but stopped abruptly and gasped. I had forgotten poor Ivan, cowering hidden beneath his cowled frock. But I felt him move suddenly, groping for something close to me, and the man saw the movement and stilled abruptly. "What's that? Near her, *there!"*

The torches steadied, and Sandra gasped in fright. Ivan was getting up slowly, an awesome figure in the executioner's hooded robe, his black mask hiding his familiar face from them, and in his hand a battleax with gold inlay gleaming on the heavy, double-edged blade. He said nothing; he just shook the ax at them and waited, moving between them and me as though in my defense. The man backed off quickly, and Sandra gave a stifled scream as her torch showed her the ax.

His silence as frightening as his looks, Ivan was a terrifying figure even to me. But the man had courage.

"We've gone too far to stop!" he muttered to Sandra. *"Kill her!* It's what you wanted to do! I'll look after *him*."

He was moving at once, with Ivan turning, watching him. He feinted with the mace and sprang back as Ivan raised his ax threateningly, and suddenly, circling right, he started laughing. "I know who you are!" he cried as though in relief. *"You poor fool!* How did *you* get involved with her?"

Sandra was holding one of the torches on Ivan, trying to blind him with its light, but frustrated by the hood and the mask. But I saw Ivan's opponent now. Briefly I saw him; disbelievingly, for it was Paul Garrick I was looking at. The chauffeur, the man Peter McDonald said worked for his father! The man I thought I could trust.

But even as he goaded Ivan, Paul Garrick had cried out in fear. He threw up his hands, the mace still gripped in one, and seemed to fall back and disappear. Sandra's torch flashed where he had been, and Sandra screamed shrilly and began backing away as Ivan turned on her.

She backed out into the passage with the torch wavering. She screamed again, a sound of pure terror, and started running back toward the museum.

Ivan followed her as far as the passage and stood there watching. He said, "They're coming, Tracey. Sandra left the stone door open so they could get back into the museum, and somebody must have seen it. They've caught her. I can see Ralph and Peter Mc-Donald."

He came back with one of the torches she must've dropped, and sat beside me.

"He fell down the mine shaft, Tracey," he said sickly. "I was only trying to stop them from hurting you again."

I said I knew that, and that he hadn't *touched* Paul Garrick. It was the man's own fault that he fell in trying to kill us. Nobody could blame Ivan, or punish him. And I held Ivan's hand reassuringly until the torches flashed into our niche in the passage wall that hid the mine shaft.

Peter reached me first. It was Peter who kissed and held me while he told me how scared he'd been when he found I was missing, and they searched the museum and saw bloodstains and the open stone door. He remembered at last that he was a doctor, which must've been something he really had forgotten, since in his anxiety he hadn't even brought me an aspirin. But he made up for that later when two of the gardeners carried me back to Glamis on an improvised stretcher. The way Peter put it, he wasn't going to allow my collection of injuries to prevent my limping to the altar with him in a few months time.

I didn't tell Peter then, but I knew I would have made it on crutches if I had to.

The rest I learned more slowly. How Sandra involved Paul Garrick by seducing and secretly marrying him, in an attempt to eliminate me from the hierarchy of the Craigs of Glamis. It was Paul Garrick who took advantage of Ivan's fantasy play in the old marshaling yard, where Ivan greased the railroad cars and moved them by leverage through the weeds. It was Paul I saw rolling the car and setting the switch. Ivan had seen him too, and was able to tell the police so.

And then there was the motive for all that horror. I still wonder about that sometimes. I still don't want to accept it. For the man I knew as my father all those years was never my father at all. I'm John Craig's daughter by blood and by marriage, conceived when my mother was still his wife and Henry Craig was many miles from Glamis, selling Craig coal in Japan.

And that, Angus McDonald informs me, makes *me* the heir apparent to the business empire of the Craigs of Glamis. Though whether I ever get it now I neither know nor care, since a doctor's wife is all I want to be.

The trouble, I think, was that others knew these things, but not poor Uncle John. . . . Sorry, my poor father. The other Craigs knew it, but were content while I, unknowing, lived in another province, until the man I thought was my father, being close to death, wrote to his brother John telling him the truth.

It brought Sandra's downfall—she is now in a mental hospital—and her husband's death. As for the other Craigs, they don't live at Glamis anymore, except for Ralph, who conducts the museum. But they all have an income that enables them to live much more comfortably in Quebec than they ever did in Glamis, thanks to my persuasion.

As for Ivan, I don't think of him as poor Ivan anymore. In some strange way, the shock of that terrible night we shared seemed to help him mature mentally, as he had physically. He no longer plays, and Ralph has only praise for his work. There are even rumors of a girl in Aberfeld, but Ivan is too shy still to talk about that. . . .

SIGNET Gothics You'll Want to Read